I0558538

REASONABLE FACSIMILE

Copyright © 2011 Chris Shella

All rights reserved. No part of this book may be used or reproduced in any manner whatsoever without written permission of the author (s) except in the case of brief quotations embodied in critical articles and reviews.

REASONABLE FACSIMILE

ISBN 978-0-9833600-4-9

REASONABLE FACSIMILE

CHRIS SHELLA

DEDICATED TO EMMALINE ELLISON SHELLA

YOU MADE ME A SUCCESS. I'LL NEVER STOP MISSING YOU.
YOU'RE THE REASON I'LL NEVER BE LIKE JD.

FOREWORD

This book is a fictional work about a lawyer on the bottom rung. This isn't allegorical. It isn't symbolic. It's just the story of a man who put other things in front of his family and himself. I hope that this book will lead you to the same conclusion that JD reached. Don't let your life be a reasonable facsimile—it must be real instead.

TABLE OF CONTENTS

PRELUDE

Cracked Bones

THE SICKENING CRUNCH OF a tooth being forced out of a jaw by a work boot was audible 50 feet from where it happened. Picture a 6'4 monster strong, malevolent, and angered, raining misery on a small 72 year old man without the strength to defend himself. Blood rolls down the streets in rivulets, coalescing on a bottle cap here and curb there. All of it fleeing the scene of the crime. Like the old man wished he could have. All the while this circus is going on; a throng of 30 + people watch this macabre dance of death. No one is doing anything to stop it. No one is doing anything to call the police. Faces mesmerized by the shattered bones and ruined shell of an old man. Sounds of agony escape destroyed lips. Mercifully, the coup de grace. A bullet snuffs out the pain, the agony, and the life of a man. With a laugh, the assailant puts away the gun, hails a hack and leaves the old man as an obscene monument to the end of life. Linwood White is dead. A murderer has fled the scene. Baltimore street justice or a reasonable facsimile?

CHAPTER 1

Call me JD

MY LIFE IS CLOSING IN on me. My heart is palpitating. My head hurts, and all I wanna do is sleep and forget the misery that is my life. I'm holding on to the bottom rung of the ladder of life and my grip is slipping. My name is Jasper Davis; I'm your friendly neighborhood defense attorney. I open my eyes and look around my studio apartment with the exposed brick walls and twenty-foot ceilings with exposed pipes. It's one of those overpriced converted factory lofts that eats my soul and the profits from my firm every day of my life. I drag myself up to one elbow and wonder, "How can I be paying a grand a month for what is essentially a room? I mean, I know I'm near the Inner Harbor of Bodymore Murdaland (a.k.a. Baltimore, Maryland), but damn, there has got to be a better way of living."

Then I think, maybe this is where divorced lawyers go to die. My wife of 15 years had kicked me out of our lovely colonial on Lake Norman in Charlotte, North Carolina because I couldn't keep Mr. Happy in my pants. I never thought I would land here. I look out my windows, which give me the lovely view of a five-level parking lot. I stretch my arms over my head as my blue and maize U of Michigan t-shirt hangs limply on my body. It's covered with drops of the grease from the steak and cheese hero I had last night. I scratch my balls though the pee slot of my shorts and groan. "Why does my body hurt so much when I'm only forty-seven years old?" I look in the bathroom mirror as I take my morning slow leak. I'm slightly balding but, in my worship of vanity, I shave my head so I look cool instead of aging. I'm not a bad looking guy, if I could smile a little more. I seem to have a slightly sad effect to

10

my face no matter what. I guess that happens when you only get to see your son once a month. He is your namesake, best friend, and raison d'être. It also happens when you realize that you threw away your life for a piece of twenty-six year old tail that wasn't worth the time it took to chase it. Oh well. I flush the toilet, and I run my bath water. Yeah, I said bath water not shower. Why can't a man soak in the tub too? That's just one of my little peccadilloes. I'm not your average forty-seven-year-old divorced lawyer. Instead of golf, I still run ball down at the YMCA. Instead of Brooks Brothers casual shirts and Dockers, I still rock throwback jerseys and Timbs (Timberlands to the uninitiated). Since today is Sunday, that is exactly what I'm gonna throw on to wear after soaking in this tub.

As I sit in the hot water, I can feel the alcohol from last night soak out of my body. Damn! How many Jack and Cokes did I have last night? My head feels like a Smurf construction worker with a teeny tiny jackhammer drilling at the base of my skull. I reach out and grab the Tylenol that I leave on the tub ledge for just this purpose. I swallow down four.

As the heat of the tub and Tylenol work on me, my mind drifts to the murder trial I will start on Monday. In my mind's eye, I see a three ring binder just with blood dripping off it. I shake my head like a wet sheepdog to take that image out of my mind. Damn, I hate the people I represent. I hate how they look. I hate how they act. I hate what they do. Defending them makes me hate myself. I walk back to my main room drip drying. I make a beeline for my open bottle of Jack. I take a deep swallow hoping it will wash the bad thoughts out of my mind. I collapse in my lazy boy and just zone out. I gotta go workout, but I have to clear my mind first.

Twenty minutes later, I'm slipping on my Michael Vick throwback jersey (fuck you PETA), a pair of Levis, and brown dilapidated Timbs with scuff marks. I set my ADT alarm system and throw on my gold slim Skagen watch that is the last present my wife bought me before she threw my unfaithful ass out the house. As I step outside, I notice the two terminally hot Asian college girls who live next door to me walking past. They greet me with smiles and waves as they walk by me and my half-locked door. I actually spend more time watching them walk away than I should, so I go past my alarm grace period. My annoying claxon goes off with my door all ajar, as I watch their assets twitch away in spandex. Thank God for Under Armour and spandex. It does an old man good. These two girls look back, giggle, and continue on their merry way. Oh well, daydreams are nice. They keep me alive and going until I have to deal with the ugliness of my reality.

I go back in, cut off the alarm, and sit down in my royal blue microfiber chair near my door. I relax and think about how I got where I am.

As I said when I first began talking to you, my name is Jasper Davis. I'm a criminal defense attorney. I represent some of the lowest forms of life on this planet. I'm no better than the hired guns in the Old West who traveled town to town killing people for money. Unlike most lawyers, I'm admitted to the practice of law up and down the eastern seaboard. So, I go state to state, fighting for justice or at least a reasonable facsimile. I wasn't always like this. I started out as a prosecutor, the man who speaks for the victims of criminals, a man who spoke for those who can't speak for themselves. But, I realized two things. First, a lot of the time, I wasn't speaking for victims; I was just speaking for the person who ran to the police first. Second, the pay for the man who speaks for those who can't speak for themselves sucks. Forty grand a year on Long Island is chicken feed. It's not enough to pay rent, pay a car note, and pay student loans . . . and it damn sure isn't enough if you wanna have some type of a social life or family. Believe it or not, I went the latter route. I got married two years out of law school. Bad decision. I should have taken the time to sow my wild oats and get to know myself as an adult. Well, fuck it. Here I am, so snap out of it. Forget your embarrassment and get on with your life.

I gather my courage, take a quick swig of Jack (hey so what if it's 10 a.m. on Sunday? Jack Daniels is the breakfast of champions), reset my alarm, lock my door, and take the stairs down out of the building. As I walk next to the garage, I reach my pride and joy-my 1994 BMW 840 CI, painted Oxford green. It is my significant other at this juncture in my life. Every middle-age man deserves a sports car. With all the shit I've been through, I deserved two fancy rides. You see, my wife got all the other cars in the divorce-my silver Chrysler 300C, my Mercedes S600, and my beloved Saab convertible. They all reside in North Carolina with my ex-wife (along with my sanity). But my BMW (the Black Man's Wish) is my baby. I just wish she had air conditioning, especially in this Baltimore summer—but I digress—I check the trunk and see that my gym bag is tucked neatly in the trunk of the car, waiting for me to go ball at the YMCA. I hop in, start her up, and hear the purr of her six cylinders. I set my Sirius satellite radio to Jamie Foxx's station as I swing thru the lot above the speed limit but below sixty. Hey, I don't wanna hurt anybody, right? I hit Baltimore Street and take a left at the corner of Mount Street. After driving through the block with its human flesh trade on display even this early, I can't stop shaking my head. The thought of paying money for AIDS doesn't appeal to me so I keep on trucking to the Y.

I pull up and park at the first parking slot I see. I run in the door as a 6'3"sister with dark complexion and tight spandex sashays past me (Are you seeing a theme with me and spandex? I'm sure you would). At the front desk, I give my membership card to the slightly dumpy college-age chocolate honey behind the counter, who always has a smile for me. Her smile is so big that eyes close when she does it. Cute. I run into the funky locker room with the nasty green carpet that looks like an elf threw up to create that color. I quickly change into my shorts and a Maize colored fab five basketball jersey. I walk into the gym and I see nine brothas and one 41-year-old snowflake running ball, five guys with shirts and four brothas without shirts, and one white boy in serious need of a tan running the point. The white boy is wearing the opposing brotha out. At 5'8"and 180 pounds, he is the shortest and slowest guy out there, but Jeff Stephens is no ordinary peckerwood—he is my main whigger on the

13

trigger. (I think he thinks the same thing about me). He has been my best friend since high school and the point guard who fed me the ball when we both played college ball overseas at the University College London. UCL baby, you already know what it is.

I grab a seat and watch as Jeff's team finishes a drubbing of the younger and bewildered brothas who can't believe the ass whopping they have suffered at the hands of this white chocolate wannabe. As the game ends with Jeff giving a no-look pass to a 6'8" accountant from Dean Witter name Josiah who slams the ball through with one hand and grabs his Johnson with another and yells "GAME" at the top of his lungs.

Jeff comes up to me and says, "Bro, what was up with that girl you left the club with last night? You must have been drunk because her mustache and goatee connected better than yours."

"Well Jeff, friends don't let friends beer goggle, so why did you let me do that?"

"Jasper, you weren't beer goggled, you were fucked up on Jack, and you don't listen to anyone when you are on Jack."

I groaned and just thanked God that I didn't wake up to her at my place. It would have been a nightmare for a bearded lady to know where I live, and I might have thrown up this morning if I had.

"Ok, ok. I gotta slow down. A bearded lady? God, I must really have been tore down by Jack." (That's Mr. Jack Daniels to you)."

Jeff says, "Come on JD." (My nickname; sorry I didn't tell you, but you wouldn't believe that my nickname is the same as initials for my favorite drink if you heard it from my mouth, right?). "Percy has got to leave. Run with us, and sweat that poison out your system. You know we gotta go over to the Baltimore jail this afternoon. You start trial on Billy's murder case tomorrow."

I groan and start stretching, thinking about William Johnson for the first time today but for the millionth time this month. Mr. William "Billy Bad Ass" Johnson is a sweetheart who "allegedly" stomped a seventy-two year old man to death over a 1990 Buick Regal. The scene was like someone had washed the sidewalk with blood. The saddest thing was how the body appeared so sad. This little old man didn't want to sit around retired; he wanted to remain active and work on what he loved. He opened a car dealership and worked on the cars himself. He sold them to local folk who needed transportation at a reasonable price. At least he did until my client came into his life and smashed his earthly shell into a bloody messy smelly pulp. I can't forget his ripped white and multicolored-striped shirt over a white undershirt so drenched in blood that you can only tell its real color by the small spots and ridges not soaked red from the old man's blood, which dripped like wet molasses from his ruined mouth onto his clothes.

Jesus! That was not an image I need right now. I shook my head to shake the Jack induced cobwebs and the nightmare inducing crime scene photos of the old man from my head. I needed to be human. Over the next two hours I worked, sweated, and dry heaved my way through game after game until sweat poured off my head like an open tap. I was tired but I felt good again. Jeff and I sat on the floor under the far basket. As I gasped and caught my breath, ten more guys ran ball and woofed at each other about "Yo man, you fouled me! Yo take this!"

"Jeff, man, none of these young boys has any fundamental skills. I don't understand how these guys who clearly played high school ball could not know how to defend a pick and roll or give and go. Didn't they ever watch tapes of Karl Malone and John Stockton from the old Utah Jazz?"

"JD, if these guys didn't see it on play station or on the AND1 Mixtape Tour, it doesn't exist to them. That's why the Europeans are filling the league. They study the game and realize it's a team sport not a one on one dunk contest."

"Yeah, I guess you're right Jeff."

"JD, are you ready for tomorrow and jury selection?"

"I will be. This case has been my whole life for the last four months, but damn, why did they have to put the case before the little general? I can't stand his sawed off Napoleonic complex ass. If he just grew four more inches, he would be a much nicer person." (Being 6' and 220 pounds of muscle, or flexible fat as my ex was bound to say, I can be an imposing figure. But the little general was a 5'3" full-of-shit judge. His fortune is owed not to his brilliant legal mind but to his dad, whose seat on the bench he inherited.) I knew he was intimidated by me, and whenever I went to a bench conference with him, he stayed on his elevated bench so he wouldn't have to look up to me. The last time I was in his courtroom, I walked out in handcuffs because I lost it after he slammed my client on a misdemeanor with consecutive time for a petty crime. I loudly said, "Thanks Dad." I thought it was just in my head or at least under my breath. The deputies told me later that I said it aloud as I pointed at the judge and laughed maniacally at him. It took the Chief Judge and the District Attorney to get me out of that. (What? That's what frat brothers are for. I-Phi till the day I die). I swear it's all a blur, but what I thought happened in my head came to life inside of Courtroom 5-2 that day.

"JD, if you can't respect the man, can't you just respect the robes? Respect the office; respect the fact that he could put your black ass in jail and subject my white ass to have to be responsible for both my own case load and yours as well?"

"Ok, ok. I'll be nice to the little sawed off mutherfucka, even though he isn't half the man his mamma was. I'll play nice. Ok Jeff?"

"Yeah, yeah, yeah. Next time he puts you in the clink, don't ask me for shit, ok?"

"Alright, I'll play nice. It's not like I have a lot to work with on this case. They've got Billy dead to rights. They can place him in the car from the dealership. His fingerprints are on the car's steering wheel. They also have two eyewitnesses who saw him beat the guy to death. He can't even testify because he's got that murder in DC that they will ask him about if he so much as dreams about taking the witness stand. But you never know. Maybe he will escape justice and the clutches of the little general, but I doubt that he will escape Lok Yao."

"Oh, wow! Lok is your prosecutor? He probably has the whole file and every time your client ever pissed on the side walk memorized."

16

Lok Yao was the number one assistant in the DA's office homicide squad. He has not only a photographic memory but also an encyclopedic knowledge (Wikipedia-like memory for all those of the internet age) of the law. He had lost cases before. Not because he was a bad lawyer, but because he had never seen a case he didn't like. He would try to convict Santa Claus of breaking and entering, even if Satan was his only witness. Lok wasn't a bad guy. He just has no sense of proportionality. He would march into hell if the police told him that it was heaven, even though he was getting jabbed in the ass with pitchforks the whole way there. That was not an issue in this case. Billy is the demon here. I wasn't sure how many bodies Billy was responsible for to date. I just guess he got so arrogant that he didn't care if people saw him kill someone in broad daylight. He hadn't been arrested in years for his violent acts in Baltimore or the surrounding areas.

As a defense attorney, it isn't my responsibility to judge my client or worry about their actions. I am mandated by law to defend my clients zealously, no matter how big a scum-sucking, shit-bucket bottom feeder they are.

I leave the gym, with Jeff's warning. I go home and open up the five 3-ring binders that contain the evidence of the last moments of Linwood White, the sad broken man in the pictures that won't leave my memory. I sat at my cheap Sauder desk that is angled to face my glorious view of the parking garage. I stretched open my mind and spent the next twelve hours of my life in the sad monument to Linwood's' life that is the prosecutor's file, the state's evidence against my client, Billy. I fell asleep in my third reading of the fourth binder. I owe it to my client. I owe it to the court system. I owe it to the son I love and to the ex whom I owe alimony to. It's my job. It's justice or at least a reasonable facsimile.

CHAPTER 2

Put Twelve in the Box and Go to the Hole

I ENTER COURTROOM 5-2 AT 9:25 a.m. Instead of the Brooks Brother suits I wore prior to the divorce, I wear the finest that Wal-Mart has to offer. I'm sporting a sharp black suit that came from the Dominican Republic; a straight-from-the-dry-cleaner's, blue, pinpoint oxford shirt; and a cheap, slightly shiny, orange tie. You can't tell me that I ain't crossing them over. I know that my whole ensemble costs less than a hundred and twenty bucks. But I look good. That suit is not likely to last past the next three months, but as far as trial goes, I'm looking sharp (at least I think I am in my own mind).

I walk through the double sets of doors that creak as I walk into the courtroom, announcing my entrance before my appearance can. The first face I see as I enter the courtroom is the little general. His face is flushed red and the steam is almost visible coming out of his ears.

He yells, "Mr. Davis why are you late to my courtroom?" I have the notice to return to court at 9:30 in my hand. As I look at the paper in my hand, the little fucker has the most evil grin on his face.

I say "Your Honor," as I hand the notice to the clerk. "The return to court notice is set for 9:30, not any earlier, and I am here before that time."

The judge says, "The local court rules state you are supposed to be here fifteen minutes before the return time for court. I know that because I posted these rules Friday evening on the court web site, and you didn't bother to read them, did you?"

I now know that I have entered my own personal hell and that for the next two to three weeks I am at the mercy of this maniac. The judge has the courtroom full of potential jurors, and he has my client looking at me from the defense table. Lok Yao is snickering into his hand at the prosecution table over to my left. But defense attorneys know that all this is par for the course. Billy is 6'5" and a former devil dog. That's right a former US marine. He has arms like tree trunks and legs thicker than transatlantic cable. He is wearing the same cheap suit that I am, but with a white shirt and no tie. It seems as if the suit is straining to hold itself together while keeping this man mountain of muscle covered by clothes as his bald head gleams in the harsh light of the courtroom.

He grabs my arm. "What the hell you doing pissing off the judge before he we even start? Mutherfucker, if you fuck me, I fuck you, bitch ass nigga," he hisses at me.

I put my arm around him and smile as I snarl in his ear, "Look bitch, this judge is trying to railroad you like I told you he would. The judge you thought was so nice is trying to bend you over and fuck you like a 2 dollar ho. So I'm your only friend in this courtroom, as I warned you before this trial started. So you best be nice to me, or what could be a life sentence will somehow become a lethal injection. Just keep pissing me off and coming at me like I'm some punk off the street." At that moment, the most God-awful smell comes from the body of this miscreant. The smell is as if five rotted skunks are sitting beside me as gas seeps out this creep as if his bowels have released. Big droplets of sweat roll down his head, and he starts shaking like a hooker in a Holiness church. He looks at me with fear in his eyes and stammers out an apology. I say, "You're welcome. Get your game face on and let's start trying to save your life."

I look at the judge and see him with a smug self-satisfied grin behind his silver wire-rimmed glasses and large nose and buck teeth. At least that's what I see when I look at him. He looks like a body double for a circus clown without the makeup. But I digress.

Now, jury selection in the state of Maryland is a user-friendly process with a few wild cards thrown into the mix. The first step is that each juror is individually screened by the judge about the answers they provided on a generic questionnaire. This form asks them about their relationship to the justice system and whether they or any one close to them has ever been a defendant or a victim. The judge sits on his courtroom throne (yeah, come on, y'all know the bench is a throne) with prosecutor and the defense attorney (moi) standing in front of him and the potential juror in between. This process repeats for each and every juror, even if they didn't have any marks on their questionnaire that would raise alarm.

So after 3 days, the first 250 jurors have been screened, and we are ready to begin the questioning by the two attorneys. The judge then directs the clerk to call 12 potential jurors into the box. Twelve jurors trudge into the box with their items with them. As they each walk by, Billy jabs me in the side and asks me what I think about that guy or that girl. Billy's bad breath smells like boiled garbage pouring into my ear and assaulting my nose. I tell him to shut up and put his impressions of each juror down on paper so I can concentrate. The jurors each steal glances at my client and me as they walk by us. Trial work is a lot like voodoo and mind reading, as I try to interpret what their body language is saying. Jury selection is part science, part observation, and part witchcraft. You are trying to pull from people a boiled-down essence of who they are within the short time that the judge gives us with the first twelve (in this case, fifteen minutes per attorney). You take that short slice of who they tell you who they are and how they will receive your client. This is nerve racking because these are the twelve people who have to judge your client's guilt or innocence and will be the same twelve who will decide if Billy Badass will live or die. Lok and I spend the next 3 days sorting through jurors who have every excuse in the world for not being able to do jury duty. It always amazes me that black folks who would never skip the opportunity to vote will find any excuse not to serve jury duty. Jury duty ensures the rights of the accused (insert any minority into that word and it's the same result). These upright citizens don't understand what disservice they are doing to our society by avoiding jury duty. They leave defendants without the chance to have people who look just like them and who have similar experiences judge them. But white folks, boyyyy, GrayBoy will go thru hell or high water to try and get on a jury and put another nigga behind bars. If the black community only understood that the duty to serve on a jury is just as important as the right to vote! How can we complain about all the black men in jail when black jurors always have a family trip or a sick cousin or a test at school that keeps them off the jury?

Now this process is called voir dire (my long tall Texan law professor called it "vour daireee"). This simply means to speak the truth. I always tell the juror that there is not a wrong answer or a right answer, only the truth (bullshit). I'm doing everything I can to trip up the people who would hate my client or me and the prosecutor is doing the same thing. So if we are asking the jury to tell the truth, we are lying to them. I listen as Lok moves workmanlike through his initial questioning. I slowly look over the first panel in the box, and I'm like, How the hell did we get a panel like this in Baltimore? I mean the city has got to be 85 percent black, and of the twelve jurors, only three are African American. Six are white, two are Asian, and one is a whigger (what is a whigger? Think Vanilla Ice and Third Bass). Lok is not a virtuoso. I mean he's not an orator, but he hits every point that he needs to. By the end of his fifteen minutes, you can see the panel members are all shaking their head in agreement with the statement he is making. Lok's magic is that he comes off as a hard working prosecutor who you want to like because he's trying to protect you and your family.

Lok grandly announces," Your honor, I'm satisfied with this panel," and shoots me a sidelong smirk, knowing I'm about to axe at least half of this panel. That will eat up half my statutory 10 preemptory strikes, which I need so that I will have a shot of even hanging the jury in this case.

"Ah, the game is afoot," I think to myself as I stride toward the jury box. I think of my fourth favorite line in cinema, "I love the smell of napalm in the morning," as I go forward to try and eliminate as many jurors as I can before I have to use my peremptory strikes. As I give my stock speech about how they are standing in a line in history from ancient Greece to the present blah blah blah blah blah, what I note is that juror 6 is an African American man who is holding a book by Bill O'Reilly entitled No Spin Zone. Shit, I'm gonna spin his ass right out the door. I then notice the cringe on juror number 3's face (a forty-something white female in a suit that is more expensive than my car, with a haircut that is frosted in place and dangling pearl earrings as big as robin eggs) as she looks at my client. Ta ta, go enjoy lunch at the country club. I see juror number 11 (the whigger dressed in Sean John jeans and a Throw Back Warren Moon Jersey playing with his tightly braided hair (my nigga; like Puff said, "You ain't goin' nowhere 'cause it's bad boy for life!"). Juror number 1 is an Asian accountant who is busily writing notes on everything that is said. I like that. That means when the prosecutor makes a promise, which Lok does every time, this guy will go back and see if he did what he promised he would. Juror number 4 is an elderly white male who is sitting in his chair with his arms crossed and glaring at me. Don't worry about me, buddy you're gone. Let me get in your ass right now.

I address juror number four with my slickest big city lawyer smile, "Mr. Phelps, have you ever been on a jury before?"

"Naw, sir. I been on a grand jury but not to trial court." Ok, this guy is smarter than I thought.

"What do you do for a living?"

"Work at Bank of America as a security guard. I'm so used to walking all day my back is hurting from sitting here all day."

"You live in what quadrant of Baltimore?" I was all prepared to hear him say South B'more, but he said, "West Baltimore for the last thirty years."

I look at his hand and I notice that his ring isn't a gold loop or a Claddagh, which is what most Irish guys like him have. It has an interlocked repeating symbol of the ankh. For the uninitiated, that is the African symbol that stands for union of man and woman. Phelps smiles when he sees me staring at his ring, and he gives an almost imperceptible nod that only a brotha would notice. I guess I misjudged him. I quickly say thank you and move on. I'm hoping and praying that Lok didn't just notice that nod. This guy wears a black man's ring, lived in West Baltimore for 30 years (the land of Marcellus Barksdale from the Wire), and knows the upward head nods that brothas give each other all day everyday (from the hood to the street to the wall street lions, they all know the upward head nod and so does Phelps). That's a brotha of another color. I'm so afraid of blowing his cover that I abruptly sit down and prepare my peremptory strikes. Lok goes first and doesn't strike anyone. I strike 3 Whites, leaving a twenty-something white female secretary who just moved into town from White Marsh. (Can't strike too many Whites, or it will put me up for a reverse Batson claim. Batson is a U.S. Supreme court case that doesn't allow peremptory strikes on a racial basis. Since I kept three, I'm ok. I also strike the Bill O'Reilly No Spin Zone reader guy and the Spanish college girl who seems not to understand English that well. That leaves seven. Mr. Phelps becomes juror number one and the default jury foreman. I'm still uneasy because Maryland has a weird rule unlike what's found in any other state. You can strike people from any part of the panel any time. You see, in every other state that I'm familiar with, these seven jurors would be safe, but not in Maryland. Lok can strike any of the seated jurors any time before jury selection ends. I can't believe he passed on my boy white chocolate, but so be it.

The judge calls for more jurors and the clerk calls five more people into the box. Four of the five are African American. The other is a twenty-year-old white Goth girl in full regalia --with the safety pin in her chin, her pale skin, black hair piled up high, the black wedding dress, and the dark mascara all around her eyes pretty much raccoon-like. Lok only asks 5 minutes of questions and sits down quickly, but he strikes two of the new African American guys who have brothers in jail for murder charges (one of whom Lok prosecuted). As that juror walks out, he ice grills Lok and calls the prosecutor a bitch ass yellow nigga under his breath. The judge calls for more jurors and two more jurors shuffle forward. Two older, heavyset Spanish women take their seats, and Lok questions them for three minutes, sits back down, and uses no strikes.

Not wanting to prolong this process and realizing that this is about to be the best racial mix I have seen. I stand up and say, "This jury looks fine to me, judge," and I sit back down. Since I didn't use any strikes, Lok doesn't get a chance to strike any more jurors and is stuck with the panel as is. Lok looks at me, pissed as hell, his face turning red. He was hoping I would strike someone because then he would have had a chance to strike some more jurors that looked to be safely on the panel. Instead, he played into my hands, and I shut the door on him. So, the twelve are seated and sworn in. We quickly pick two alternates.

The judge calls me and Lok to the bench and says, "I'm gonna be away for a long weekend, so court will be adjourned 'til Monday, and we will then proceed with opening statements." Man, you don't know how glad I was.

CHAPTER 3

An evening out

SO, FOR ONCE I have an early weekend. I just don't know what to do with myself. I could go down to the Inner Harbor and try to pick up a professional woman or go to Streakers and pick up a twenty year old hood chick, or I could go home cry and try and pick up the pieces of my life. See, what you have to know about me is that just below the surface there is a lot of melancholy in me a lot of sadness, a lot of regret. I married a woman I probably shouldn't have married, stayed with her at first because of inertia and then because we had a son, Jasper Junior. I loved her as a friend but not as a wife. I mean when you're married to someone and you don't have sex for 7 years, can you still be romantic about them? But my problem is that I lost respect and therefore lost my mind and rarely saw an ass I didn't like. I chased brown, black, Spanish, and white girls like I was still in college. Until one day it caught up with me, when a particularly vindictive woman decided that the key to her happiness was breaking up my family, so that I could be with her. She told my wife everything after being on some fatal attraction shit. Well, she will have the next three years to think about that at the local Women's Correctional Facility in Raleigh. I still lost my wife, my ability to see my son every day, and most of my worldly possessions and toys.

I decided that, instead of moping around, I would go hear some jazz at a spot on Hopkins Street near the Harbor. I really didn't want any company. I just wanted to wash the film of the filth that had settled on my mind just from having been in close proximity to Billy the Badass old man stomper.

I walk to the club that is a five minute walk from the Clarence Mitchell Courthouse where I have been on trial all week. My nerves were frazzled like a blooming onion and my spirit was low. I walked past the CVS drugstore and stopped at the distinctive, reflective doors of the Shake House Jazz Bar.   Just inside the door way, there was a doppelganger of Carmen Jones all the way to the red flower behind her right ear. She greets me with a sweet, lilting voice that is so melodic I don't even mind the twenty-five dollar admission she requests from me. She could have asked me for an Audi TT convertible with the optional turbo and I would have handed that over just as easy. I give it up like I'm in a trance. Just then, I look at her left hand, fourth finger, and see a plain gold wedding band. I may be a leech, but I respect the institution of marriage, even if I didn't respect my own. I smiled, walked to the bar, and sat on a worn red topped cushioned bar stool that ran the length of the bar that was approximately 40 feet long. The stage was directly across from the bar, a good 50 feet away across a space littered with tables and people laughing. Everyone was having a good time as a jazz trio played. I seemed to be the only lone wolf in the bar. So, I turned back to the bar with its reflective mirror behind it. I picked up a dog-eared menu and started to peruse what was gonna be the only things I was gonna eat tonight. That's because none of these ladies looked like they were gonna cooperate with my program, especially since they all had their husbands and boyfriends with them. I'm not into the group thing ya know. So I settle on the well-done rib eye steak, butterflied, and a baked potato loaded with cheddar cheese, bacon, sour cream, chives, and butter, with a vegetable medley.

For the next 35 minutes, my attention keeps being pulled back to my "Carmen." As I slowly wash three Jack and Cokes down my throat, I guess I took one too many sidelong glances because when I look up to peek at her again, she turns and looks at me. I quickly put my head down and swallow more Jack and Coke. I crunch down on a piece of ice. I then look back up and there she is still looking back at me. This time she smiles.... my heart palpitates so fast I think that maybe I need to see a

26

cardiologist. I give a weak smile and wave that took the strength of AJAX (for you uninitiated, you should read about the Trojan Wars and the Greek heroes therein. Reading is fundamental.) just to execute those maneuvers. The momentum of my wave was just a little too much for my stool perch and it tilts up and my ass slides to the ground hard. I quickly jump up but my face is hot with embarrassment. "Real cool, jackass!!" I think to myself. I remount the stool and hang my head down. I peak at her and she is laughing. I quickly look down and back at my drink. My face is burning hot without any sort of grace. I can't believe she caught me staring at her and I fell on my ass. My food arrives mercifully and I concentrate on that steak - perfectly well-done no pink at all. I slather A1 sauce on it and don't even mention that they forgot the chives. All I want to do is concentrate on the music. The smooth sounds of Najee are in my ear. I just want to cool my damn face off and regain my cool points. About 7 minutes into the meal, I feel a soft feather-light touch on the nape of my neck. At first I mistake it for a draft from the air conditioning because it's the softest touch I have ever felt. I turn around and "Carmen Jones" smiles in my face. I'm stunned and I feel like a grade school kid who just passed a note to the prettiest girl in school hoping she'll check the yes box and be his girlfriend.

You would think as a big time trial lawyer that talking is the thing that comes easiest to me. But, the way I figure it, as you walk into the courthouse, an unseen hand reaches down and turns your motor mouth switch on. As you leave, the same hand turns that sucker off. If I could just get out of the courthouse someday with it on, maybe I could talk to a beautiful woman. But as it now stands, I'm a bumbling idiot around the fairer sex.

Carmen reaches out her hand and says, "Hi, my name is Carmen," with the softest lilting Haitian accent I have ever heard. Wow. It takes me three full seconds to realize that she wants me to shake her hand. I scramble to regain my composure and in my rush I slip off my three foot high bar stool and land loudly straight on my ass and my head whips back and hits on the back of the stool's long metal stand and it is good night Charlotte. I awake in what seems like an instant to the loudest laughter I have ever heard. Even the band has stopped playing so they can laugh at my uncoordinated ass. But she doesn't laugh. Carmen is on one knee with my face cupped by her hands, and she asks, "Are you ok?" I smile which causes me to wince because the back of my head feels like the time a client of mine hit me in the back of the head with a chair when he was convicted of child molesting. (Good riddance of bad rubbish)... but I digress.

"I'm ok. I guess I've never been greeted by an angel before and it startled me." She gives a wide toothy smile that reveals her pearly white teeth and deep dimples that a man could get lost in. Carmen has a medium to light brown complexion with glasses and a medium bob hairstyle that is feathered and frames her face. Her bod is that of a Goddess. 5'7", maybe 137 pounds. Flat stomach not washboard abs but a little pleasing softness to it. Round hips and a cute cheerleader's butt. Her arms are smooth and sculpted and her cleavage is a nice 34 C cup. Simply the most beautiful woman I ever met. She helps me to my feet as the band restarts but the song they play is "Whoops there Goes Another Rubber Tree Plant." I guess it's in my honor.

I regain my worn red leather stool cushion and she perches on the one next to me. I say "Hi I'm Jasper, but my friends call me JD. That's Mister Jack Daniels to you." I give off a sickly laugh.

She smiles and says, "I'll give you a clue. You don't have to try so hard. I walked over here to meet you because I'm interested. Relax, talk to me, and be yourself. You got your foot in the door without saying a word. Don't continue to use silly lines, or I'll have to shut that door in your face."

I gulp, take a sip of my Jack and Coke and I turn back around to her and I say in my plainest, resigned voice, "Hi, I'm Jasper Davis, Carmen, and it's a pleasure to meet you. So where are you from? Your accent and name says Haiti to me."

Carmen smirks "Now that wasn't so hard to be genuine was it, chère. Yes, I'm Haitian. S'il est passé. And you Cher... where are you from?"

"I'm from North Carolina. I'm a country boy... just a black man trying to survive in a cold and harsh world."

Carmen says, "There you go again, talking in clichés."

"Baby, it's hard not to talk in clichés when my life is one bad cliché. In fact it is a cautionary tale. I'm the physical evidence of what happens to a promising lawyer who doesn't live up to his promise. I once was a good man and knew what it was to be a good man. Now I'm just a hack paying rent and alimony... one case melds into another... I don't feel like I'm doing justice¼ it's just a Ferris wheel going round and round... the best I can say I do in my work is a reasonable facsimile of justice. I have a reasonable facsimile of life period."

"Wow, that's a mouthful. So is that why you always have that sad puppy dog look on your face every time I see you?"

"Every time you see me? I've never seen you before and that may be my loss. But when have you ever seen me before?"

"I guess you never noticed the quiet, bookish lawyer with her hair pulled back in misdemeanor court. Or when I sat in and watched you try several cases before." My face begins to burn crimson with the heat of embarrassment that is filling me up ... I have seen her before and, in fact, when I was summing up in trial I looked at her one time like she was the only person in the room. I gave part of my argument directly to her. She had on thick black chunky glasses, no makeup, and a severe blue suit with a white blouse. I thought she was gorgeous then, and my mack daddy meter had gone off but, by the time the judge had finished charging the jury, she was gone. The look of recognition and surprise on my face made her laughter tinkle out of her. She said, "You don't expect me to wear my work clothes in the evening?", as she gives my now rumpled black trial suit a once over and says " or maybe you did since it seems to be your style."

I laugh and say, "It's not my style but at this time in my life I have sort of stopped caring. There is no one left to impress and I have learned to tolerate my own company... what's your story Carmen?"

"Well," she relates, "I was born in Haiti in a small village on the coast. My parents were part of the small middle class, which was amazing considering their brown skinned complexion there. My father and mother were educated in England at Kings College and wanted a better life for our family. So when I was nine, we moved to the United States. I grew up in Westchester County, New York. My father worked as a professor at Columbia and my mom was an investment banker. I was the only child, so I was pretty much spoiled but still very conservative because of my catholic upbringing. I went to all-girls schools until college. I went to NYU where I got to experience life. I met so many different types of people even though I still lived at home. I then went to Hofstra Law School. I was good at writing motions but not so good at speaking on my feet. I wanted to work myself and have my own practice. So after graduation, I put out a shingle and started my own little immigration and misdemeanor criminal defense practice." During that long dissertation, I was unable to interrupt because I swear I saw a light emanating from her eyes. I swear it. This is no bullshit, gentle reader, this girl's eyes actually emitted light. Damn I was in love or something close to it... I relayed my tale of woe to her from my graduation, law school, marriage, divorce, how my son was my hero and best friend, and how I lived now that I was alone... As the conversation wore on my eyes slowly drifted back to the gold band on the ring finger of her left hand and it froze there. I wondered as this girl was saying all the right things why she hasn't yet said anything about being married. I mean that is a gold band right? It's not like she just wanted to go out and buy herself a big diamond just to have showy jewelry. She is wearing a simple band to signify her marriage and has yet to say anything to me about it.... so as we sat there I still had an enraptured look on my face and in my words but my heart was sinking down to the top of my Stacy Adams boots.

Do I push the issue if she brings it up? Do I bring it up? Or do I wait for her? I mean, if I bring it up, I look pushy. If she brings it up, I can listen as a concerned gentleman. The last thing that I think is typical of being a defense attorney: Is she just having a fantasy conversation one evening in a club then she will disappear from my life forever?

Do I glance hard, I mean, make my whole head point to her ring to see if she reacts.... or do I touch it and play with it when I hold her hand. Maybe that will bring it to her attention.

"Jasper? Why are you distracted? Your face looks like there is a whole conversation going on in your head in the middle of our conversation. I hate it when a man doesn't truly listen to me. I hate it when a man just gives the conversation those comforting words that make most women believe that someone is actually listening to them."

Damn? She knows the male listening sounds gambit? Damn. I guess not too much gets pass this woman....

"Carmen, we've talked about so much this evening. I've told you about my life my ex and my son. I've told you about my pain and sorrow but all you've told me so far is information that stops short of the door of your home. I want to get to know you and I want you to like me. But I need to know who you are too. I mean beyond just being a lawyer or the door girl at a jazz club. A furrow wrinkled her brow and it seemed like the words "trouble" and "sadness" and "pain" were written on her face with a permanent black magic marker. She wasn't mad. She seemed resigned to her fate...

"Jasper, do you really want to hear about my sad life or do you want the pretty girl who made you laugh and smile tonight in your bed?"

"Any man would want you for his bed, any man would want you for his wife, but I ask why is there such a gap in getting to know you." She touches my face again and says "I will tell you in time but I'm not ready yet. This is the first time we talked and I'm not ready to let any man into my heart yet, especially not a slick talking lawyer." I start to protest. She puts her index finger which smells like heaven and tastes like honey on my lips and says "Hush. You'll get to know me but in my time, ok?" She slips me her business card: Carmen Jones, Esq. She stands up, kisses my forehead, and sashays away as her hips bump side to side in her tight skirt like a coconut tree swaying in a tropical wind.

31

I slowly drain the glass of my fifth Jack and Coke, pull on my trial suit jacket and I walk to the door and head to my house five blocks away. I look at my watch. I was in there for 6 hours and 5 of them were spent with Carmen..... As I walked to the loft, I looked at the stars and since I was in Baltimore I had to look around the street and keep my awareness as I walked up Light St.... they don't call it Bodymore Murdaland for nothing. Point blank, I don't want to be the 255th victim of the year as the Baltimore City paper declared the 254th victim in yesterday's weekly publication. I got to my door, unlocked it, and collapsed on my bed and slept a dreamless drunken blissful sleep - with the card of Carmen Jones clutched tight in my hand under my chin like I held the toy hot wheels cars my mom gave me when I was a kid.

CHAPTER 4

Opening Statements

I SPENT THE REST of the weekend looking at Carmen's card and reviewing the case file of Billy Badass. Now, on Monday morning, I drink my morning coca cola for my shot of caffeine. I don't eat breakfast once a trial starts.

I haven't since my first jury trial of a shoplifting case in 1997. It's just that I can't keep food down when trying a case. Trials cause balls of stress in my head, tightness in my throat, and sweat on my brow... that's not a good combination with eggs and bacon. It's a recipe for throwing up which is exactly what I did five minutes before the judge called that case for trial. My mouth tasted sour all day and I was petrified that I had chunks of eggs, grits, and tiny pieces of bacon all over me....now the only thing that happens when I don't eat is that my bowels loosen instead but I can handle that ... I don't think there will be chunks of feces on me.. The hunger edge makes my hearing keener, my eyes sharper, and my instincts better. Like a caveman on the prowl, I can beat down the prosecution on an empty stomach and eat them as my prey hehehehe. Primal image huh? Not pretty, but criminal justice isn't pretty.

Some courts—think the federal court—present a courtly stage where it is like the Supreme Court trial process. But in my mind, they are wrong. A trial is a street fight. You bring a knife; I bring a bat. You bring a bat; I bring a pistol. You bring a pistol; I bring a bazooka. You bring a bazooka; I will cause a nuclear holocaust up in this piece.

That's a trial to me. And in my business of homicide defense, a man's (usually they are male) life is at stake. This morning is opening statements, and that's like the wolf or the bragging session before the fight starts. You know where the players call each other all sorts of motherfuckers and bitches and talk about the other's mother's sexual proclivities.

You see, all an opening statement is, is when one motherfucker gets up (read prosecutor) and says how he is gonna prove that you, bitch (read defendant), ain't shit; he is gonna prove that that bitch ain't shit, and that that punk motherfucker over there (read defense attorney) can't do shit about what I'm saying, even though his lying ass will try, and when the dust clears, I'm gonna lay both those mark ass bitches down. Then the natural badass (read defense attorney) gets up and says that the lying ass motherfucker that just spoke is full of shit, that he ain't shit, his mama (read prosecutor's office) ain't shit, and his boys (read police department) ain't shit either. And that after all these bitch made snitch ass motherfuckers (read witnesses), you gonna have to realize that this nigga beside me is righteous and let those scheming ass punks (prosecution team) that you know they're lying by signifying on them (read giving a verdict of not guilty). And, oh yeah, the judge is the instigator who is saying, "Baddest one hit my hand."

So I walk down from my loft to the street. I had my satchel over my left shoulder and my trusty Dell XPS m140 computer in it. I'm ready to go to war. I walk quickly but I have to remove my jacket because it is sweltering out here and the heat is pounding down. The air is thick enough to cut through with a butcher knife. But the benefit is that all the women you see are wearing short skirts and light blouses. The college girls all have on shorts and wife beater tees on or midriff shirts. I enjoy the view on my four block walk to the Clarence Mitchell Courthouse. I clear security quickly with my green State of Maryland Bar id card. I walk up the ornate marble stairs to the courtroom. You could never imagine that a place so full of ugliness like a courthouse can be so full of beauty....ornate marble stairs... frescoes and bas reliefs of Roman and Greek figures, ornate oil paintings of judges past and two hundred year old chandeliers.... all this pomp and circumstance for something so cruel and inhuman as crime and justice – it's man at his ugliest dressed up at his prettiest.

As I walk into Courtroom 5-2 I have a surprise because instead of the little general on the bench, there is Judge P., the senior judge of the criminal division. Judge P. is a black man of about 58 years of age. He has a dark brown complexion and a short haircut with his hair more pepper than salt. He has a well-trimmed goatee connecting to his moustache. He has a perpetual half smile on his face as if he has a joke he heard that no one else knows ... he is perpetually amused by us mere human beings but he is a good man and a good judge. Judge P., says "What's wrong Mr. Davis? Were you expecting the Little General? "

"Well, yes sir. I did Judge P."

"I guess you didn't see the papers this morning?" Judge P. reaches the newspaper over the bench and says come take a look at this... On the front page there is the Little General in his tighty whites and horn rim glasses being drug out to a police car with the caption "Judge caught with his britches down." My jaw drops to the floor as I grabbed the paper with two hands and read that the Little General was caught getting a blowjob in the back stairways of the courthouse by court officers on Friday after work.... by an Asian transsexual who was on probation to him.... naughty naughty oh well....

Judge P. say the Little General got caught with his little general out... And smirks... heaven has blessed me or at least William Johnston a.k.a. Billy Badass will get a fair trial.

I set my bag down noticing that my client is looking at me confused and sweating bullets. He's sweating so heavy that both his pits are stained with sweat through his white oxford shirt. "What's going on JD.... where is the white boy judge? He looked kind and understanding. I thought he was my friend he spoke so kind to me all the time."

I look at him and say "Yeah dumbass he was picturing his cock in your mouth. He wasn't being nice, he just wanted a clean record that showed how nice he was to you before he started fucking you over on every ruling and sentencing you to double life plus four hundred years...

35

this judge is the best in the courthouse, one of the best I have been in front of and that includes the whole eastern seaboard..."

"SORRY SORRY Mr. Davis I'm just nervous ... you know I've never been on trial before."

"Yeah, right." I gritted my teeth and thought that's only because the witnesses never lived to make it to the trial before with your homicidal tendencies ass.

I plopped down and opened up my Dell laptop which I nicknamed Road Warrior because it is almost as nicked up scratched and grizzled as I am. One day I'm gonna sit down and bang out the great American novel on this bad boy and leave all this trial work shit to the young guns.... I open up three new yellow legal pads, place three Skilcraft Alpha Elite Gel pens next to them... run my computer while its Windows XP system loads (fuck Vista). My computer whirs and sighs like it is about to give up the ghost but finally it loads and up pops my trial outline of my opening statement.

I rustle around some more while Lok Yao wanders in with his lead case detective, Det. Sgt. Williams from the homicide division. Williams looks exactly like detective Bunk from the WIRE tv show ... so much that he even gets asked for autographs. He's a heavyset brotha about five feet 8 inches with a mini-fro. He has a thick short mustache and baritone voice with a tendency to curse at a minute's notice as calmly as others would say hello... But he is a friendly sort and he doesn't curse to intimidate, he curses to communicate his feelings on an issue like that prosecutor sure is a cocksucking faggot or that cop is from the bitch ass rat squad. You know, for emphasis. He looks at me winks an eye. Head is my nigga. We used to troll the nightclubs for strange (once again for the uninitiated: strange is pussy that is new to you and you wanna get to hump on it that evening) together. Boy that brotha goes for the gusto. He won't go for the single mom out for a night of fun or the college girl looking for a sugar daddy. That nigga goes for the fashion model visiting on assignment type bitch. He really goes for the gusto and once or twice

I'll be damned if he didn't get that shit....I myself tend toward the young dumb college girl looking for a sugar daddy except I'm a little low on sugar account of my ex-honey bee, my wife, makes sure through child support and alimony that my sugar is at a fucking minimum. But I digress.

Back to the subject at hand, Head and Yao set up at the prosecution tables for opening statement. The clerk is a heavyset, redbone sistah... with freckles and reddish tinted up do. She has a pleasant gap tooth smile. I have often thought of putting that gap to use but I snap back to attention as the jury pours in. Judge P. announces to the jury that he is taking over the case from here. He orders the jury not to speculate about the absence of the prior judge and that it was time to listen to the opening statements of counsel. First goes Lok. He walks his thin frame over to the bar and sort of looms over it. (Too close in my estimation. I can tell that by how the jurors right in front of him look startled and rear back away from Lok. He is blissfully ignorant of that as I snicker.) He starts his opening in a normal rich tone that seems out of place for his lanky Asian frame. That voice should be coming out of a 6ft 220 pound brother with a shaved head not a skinny Asian kid. Lok starts "Ladies and Gentleman of the jury, my opening is essentially a roadmap to what I will prove in this case. The defendant William Johnson (street-name "Billy Badass") decided on the 9th day of June 2009 that he had the right and ability to take the life of Linwood "Blackshoe" White... beating him in the head with a tire iron breaking several bones in his body causing his brain to hemorrhage and swell. AND THE COUP DE GRACE WAS A BLAST TO THE HEAD WITH A .40 caliber silver-plated Smith and Wesson handgun. This was a brutal case of overkill. The medical examiner will tell you that the beating was sufficient to cause the death as was the gun shot. Linwood was 5 ft. 5 inches and a hundred and forty pounds. He was a 72 year old man who simply told Billy Badass "no" when he asked to borrow his car, a 1990 Buick Regal. Nothing fancy, nothing exotic, just an old regal but it was Linwood's pride and joy. And because he stood up to Billy Bad, that car was the end of him. In this case, I will prove to you that William Johnson a.k.a. Billy Badass took the life of a 73 year old man with a brutal beating and a gunshot to the head without provocation. That he took that man's life not just because of a car but because this little old man did something that no one else ever had. He told Billy Badass "no" to his face. Thank you for your time and attention."

Judge P. says to the jury "Now the jury will hear from the defense. Mr. Davis you have the floor."

I sit for thirty seconds. I stare at the jury and they stare at me. I fold my glasses and slowly rise to my feet. I button the top button on my three button black Brooks Brother suit, shoot my cuffs on my crisp white laundered shirt and smooth my maize golden tie (Go Wolverines!). I slowly pace toward the lectern, set my notes down on the top of the light brown wood. I glance at them then fold them in two and step to the side of the lectern and lean against it with my right elbow as if I'm resting against a bar at the local saloon

In a clear crisp voice I say, "Wow. If all of what the prosecutor says is true then why are we here? I mean Wow. But guess what ladies and gentlemen, you are the sole judge of the facts. No one else is. His honor is the judge of the law. You are the judge of the facts. That is not my role or the persecutors role. Sorry, I meant prosecutor's role. That job is solely the domain of the jury. That means you ladies and gentleman."

"I'm going to be brief but I ask you to listen to the facts, listen to the time line, and listen to what the disinterested witnesses have to say... listen to the people who have nothing to gain or lose and don't have an interest. I ask that you let them be your guide. "Now I'm gonna sit down but I tell you that, at the end of this case, I will talk to you again and ask you to come back with the only verdict consistent with the credible evidence in this case. The only verdict that is consistent with justice, a verdict of Not Guilty."

I turned on my heel stride back to my desk and the judge turns to Lok and barks "First witness, counsel."

Lok rises to his feet and says "I, the State of Maryland, call Laquaana Richardson." The bailiff opens the front door to the courtroom and calls out "Laquaana Richardson." In strides a honey golden complected black woman of about 5'4" in a bright flowery summer dress. Her blonde hair is in dreads (for some people dreads are only a fashion choice not a statement on their life and values. It's about the same thing as choosing Levis versus Wrangler jeans) which are pulled back into a pony tail secured at the nape of her neck with a twist. I wonder to myself does she look so sweet and virginal when she walks into work at Norma Jeans on the block each day. (For the uninitiated once again, the block is the armpit of Baltimore - it is actually two blocks of strip clubs and sex shops near Baltimore's Inner Harbor. It's what passes for adult entertainment. What it really is, is drug infested, disease infested, and full of drug dealers and pimps and petty thieves. They'll steal everything from your shoes to your life if you give them the chance. I've gone there infrequently but I don't like AIDS with my lap dances. Sorry but I'm finicky like that. Laquaana strides to the stand like she is a schoolmarm walking to the head of a classroom... what type of freaky lessons she was going to teach? I have no idea. I glance sidelong at Billy and he looks sheepishly back at me... His taste in women is about to bite him in his ass. Laquaana is his girlfriend who decided to testify against him. This way she won't go to jail for the 5 kilos he had stashed at her apartment. The drugs were found when the police knocked down the door to her brick townhouse in the Brooklyn section of Baltimore to arrest his black ass. Laquaana isn't just staring daggers at Billy but axes, guns, howitzers and about every other piece of weaponry that can be conceived. I thought I saw her stare Luke Skywalker's light saber in one of her looks... damn that's an evil stare when it includes make believe weapons.

Lok asks her name and what section of Baltimore does she reside in. She says in a perfect imitation of Minnie Mouse, "Laquaana Richardson and I live in Brooklyn section." Wow, I thought no matter how sexy she is I couldn't have listened to that voice for five minutes after I busted a nut but it takes all types. I look at Billy and this huge guy seems to be shrinking in his chair at my look of disapproval. This guy was a violent asshole but he was rich enough to pay my $200,000 retainer of which half went to my partner and 80 grand went to my ex as alimony to keep my black ass out of jail. So he could have afforded a better quality woman but I guess accountants and doctors aren't clamoring for psychopathic killer drug dealers. We settle in and I object occasionally to the questions. I don't object to the legality of the questions. I object just to throw off Lok's rhythm. I'm a sweetheart, ain't I? Laquaana drones on about how violent Billy was and how he beat her the day of the killing (which makes it relevant to you junior wannabee lawyers). She relates how they were walking down Delmon St. when Billy commented on the pretty Buick Regal off to the right. It was "shiny and with chrome rims and old" in the words of Laquaana. Laquanna says that she didn't see the big deal but Billy couldn't stop talking about it. He walked directly over to it. The next thing she knew, she heard Billy yelling at someone and someone yelling back at him but nowhere near the volume Billy had... Laquaana decided that she'd rather go ahead and get her nails done. She walks away. So goes the testimony of Laquanna.

I think for a moment but I pass on asking any questions. Laquaana gets up from the stand. She does her slinkiest walk towards the gallery. She immediately sits beside a muscular white male dressed all in black, black sweater, black pants, black belt, and black eyeglasses. She wraps her arms around his left arm and lays her head on his shoulder grinning at Billy. Yep she is now with GrayBoy, Mr. GrayBoy... the local white gangster/pimp/drug dealer and Billy's main rival. Damn! That was low. Testify and give the pussy away to a white boy. Damn! It don't get no lower than that.

Lok then calls a procession of uniform police officers. They testify to absolutely nothing of value. One guy talks about standing on the perimeter of the crime scene. One talks about how he hooked up the victims vehicles and loaded it on the tow truck. Lok didn't call them for their evidentiary value he called them so the jury would see these young earnest officers troop in and impress the jury by sheer volume of witnesses. The jury won't remember their testimony just that they were there. It's not a bad strategy but you run the ultimate risk: the risk of boredom. You risk the ultimate problem of the jury falling asleep and shutting down so much that they won't pay attention to your important witnesses, the ones you want them to hear. But I'm not in the business of telling a persecutor, (oops there I go again), I mean prosecutor, how to convict my client. So, the next two days proceed with an endless parade of faceless cops and crime scene techs that each did a minute piece of work in this case. By 5:00 on Wed. afternoon, Lok calls his last drone. I look at the list of witnesses the state must provide the defense. This lets me know that it will be time for real witnesses tomorrow morning. Then Judge P. admonishes the jury to keep an open mind. Judge P. tells the jury not to discuss the case with anyone and then calls it a day. He leaves the bench and the courtroom clears out pretty quickly. Head and Yao head out. The DOC officers come over and hook Billy up and his constant refrain is "How are we doing, Mr. Davis?" "How is everything going for me?" "Davis, are we winning?" ""Is it close?" Blah blah blah blah blah. When defendants whine it all runs together in my mind. These big bad thugs are gangsta until their ass is before a judge. It puts in my mind the adage my mommy told me when I was a little boy "If you weren't such a devil during the day, you wouldn't be so afraid at night". Soon the courtroom is emptying out and all that's left in there is my dusty self and the bailiff. He keeps looking at his watch. He keeps looking at me and grimacing. I say, "Ok, ok, ok. I'm outta here." I drop my laptop in my worn leather bag and shove the papers in, not even caring to sort them. I'm just dog tired and ready to get out of there.

CHAPTER 5

Goodnight Norma Jean

AS I WALK OUT of the courtroom, I take a hard left and go down the stairs to the front of the courthouse. I burst out the front door. As I walk down the steps I see a little clump of misery as somebody's home is sold at auction. I see a grandmotherly black woman looking sad with five little ones around her legs clinging on. God, this courthouse is a place of misery. I have got to get the fuck out of here. I walk down the street and take a left. I know where I am headed without announcing it to myself and within a few minutes I have entered the BLOCK. I see the armpit of Baltimore but today I need to be enveloped in it. I walk into the first bar on the right and start my club crawl where I go from club to club looking for a sexy woman to have fun with. I end up in Norma Jeans. Norma Jeans is the sexy black girl club where the music is hot and the assets are fat. No offense to white girls. There has been a plethora of white girls with black girls' asses lately, but nothing gets a brother going like a cornbread fat ass. I guess we are all becoming genetically closer by just being around each other. I have seen some white girls that put sisters to shame. I walk in and sit at the bar right near the register. I sip on the Jack and Coke that the red-boned bartender in the ripped striped jeans and tube top shirt just made for me. Man, the drink slows everything down and brings me back to life. I look at the two girls gyrating on stage. One is about 5'4" dark chocolate with 34 B cup breasts but with an ass built to be worshiped. The other is a light bright sister about five ten with multi colored braids in her hair. She is currently sliding down the pole upside down with her legs extended like she is waiting on a bed for her lover to mount her missionary style. R. Kelly's "Twelve Play" is playing in the background. That is my favorite strip club song because it is long and strong and makes the girls grind harder. I lean back in my chair and exhale the filth of the courtroom from my lungs. I light a Cohiba that I smuggled into the country from my last visit to the Dominican Republic. I call it the DR. Damn! The DR has the sexiest women and best cigars. After the stress I've been through today, this feels like Heaven. I ask the bartender for change for a hundred dollar bill. She gives me all ones. I'm set for a good night. I might not be able to make it rain but I damn sure can make it drizzle. Minutes become hours. Around 10 pm, I move to a table where I get another hundred ones. Pocahontas appears before me. Pocahontas is a sister with a medium brown skin tone wearing a brown buckskin skirt and buckskin halter top. She has straight black hair in two braids down each side of her head. The Indian style ensemble is topped with a leather head band with a single feather attached to the back of her head. I'm hypnotized. She sits down and smiles at me. Just at that moment my phone rings and guess what? It's Carmen Jones. Ok, it's Carmen but I can dream can't I. This is not a good look. I couldn't answer and let Carmen hear the booty shaking music. By now MC Hammer's Pumps and a Bump is playing. No. I could let it ring and let her think I was ignoring her. I choose the coward's route and let the phone ring through to voice mail. I need an Indian scalp tonight not a dreamboat. Pocahontas asks me to buy her a drink so I oblige. She looks at me over the straw to her forty dollar drink of soda and purrs. "What do yo do fo a living? I always see you spending a grip in here. You could be spending that money on me instead". I say "I agree. What time do you get off?" She says, "I could leave now if you pay my tip out fee of 150 and you could do whatever you want with me." After my day in court, that is just up my alley. I say "ok" and she smiles, jumps up, and goes and runs and gets her manager. A six foot four swarthy brotha with dreads walks up and asks "Do you want to pay for this young lady's tipout????" I say "Hell yeah." I reach for my wallet and start to take out cash but I realize I'm divorced so it really doesn't matter what the fuck appears on my credit card so I pull out American Express. It's everywhere I want to be, like up in this tight ass coochie. He swipes and I sign the receipt while this is going on Pocahontas runs into the back and is dressed and waiting at the table the second the receipt pops out. We walk out of the club together. She wraps the belt of her shiny plastic green jacket around her. She purrs, "Daddy where is your car?" "Baby, it's at the crib. We are only 4 blocks away." "But daddy I don't wanna walk." she protests. And I think about it. This is Baltimore after 10 o'clock and do I really want to walk. I just dropped $300 in that club. I'm sure a lot of eyes beside Pocahontas' were on me as well as some eyes that were hungry. Some want what I got in my pocket to be in their pocket. So since discretion is the better part of valor, I quickly hail a cab that promptly tries to put me on a grand tour to pump up the volume of the fare. I promptly tell him I'm gonna report him to the hack commission. He then turns off the meter and accepts five bucks for the fare. He pulls up to my building which is right across from the Mariner Arena. I'm home. Home sweet Centrepoint. Pocahontas' mouth drops open as she looks at the apartment. "Wow u live here daddy? Wow," she repeats as we walk in and take the elevator. I unlock the door to my kingdom and Pocahontas is fully wet and her nipples are clearly erect. I have heard about gold diggers, but my little studio actually had this girl aroused. As we walk in, she looks around and says, "I love your apartment, Daddy. Damn this is sexy." I flop down on my overstuffed comfy leather chair. She comes over and sits in my lap and says "Wow, Daddy, are you a baller? I love this spot. It's ok. I gonna show you how grateful I can be to you Daddy. I'm gonna make you feel so good, you gonna want me to move in." She undoes her coat and drops to her knees. The next thing I know my dick is enveloped in soft warm wetness. This isn't a porno book so let's just say that "IT'S ALL GOOD!!!!!!!!!!!!!!!!!" I love it when a woman is a screamer. I wake up the next morning and this girl is in jeans and a blue halter top with her hair tied in a ponytail. She's in the kitchen making my breakfast! She says "Good morning sweetheart. How are you doing? Do you like your eggs soft or well?" I groggily reply, "well done" and glance over at my clock which says six o'clock. I groan and roll over.... she says "I hope you don't mind but I wanted to show you that I'm a good girl. Just because I dance and have 4 kids by four baby daddies doesn't mean I'm not a good girl." What? I think to myself. What the fuck have I stuck my dick in? She says my name is Trina. "What's your name?" I say, "Billy .... "Billy? That's not what's on your license. Jasper, why are you trying to play me???? Daddy that's not right." I groan inside. Now how the hell am I gonna get rid of this girl. I gotta be in court in three hours and I don't need happy Pocahontas the hooker in my kitchen. She says "I hope you like bacon, sausage, and grits. I want to make you happy?" I drag myself to the bathroom and look at my blood shot eyes in the mirror. I wonder why the hell did I bring this girl to my apartment? This is not good. I brush my teeth. I gargle. I dry shave. Then brush my teeth again. By the time I come out again my table is set and the food smells delicious. Damn. I sit down and take a bite. Trina aka Pocahontas says "I hope you like it. I wanna show you I can be good to you." The breakfast takes like it was made by my momma back home in NC. I grub everything while she sits there. She watches me grub the food. I tell her "Thank you baby girl. What is your story? I can't believe that there aren't fifty guys at your doorstep trying to take care of you." She smiles sadly and says, "There are plenty of guys that want to sleep with me, but none who want to be a real man and help me with my responsibilities." I ask her, "Well, if you have four baby daddies that should be a gang of child support that should make life easier." She says "Man those niggas don't help. My children belong to me. They don't have no daddies. Only punk ass sperm donors." I ask, "Where do you live?" She replies, "I live with my mom and she watches my kids when I work at night. I gotta go get them. I just wish I could meet a nice guy like you to be there for me." I'm listening to her. Shit my mind is racing. Is there a way I can keep this woman around as my dick woman? (For the uninitiated that is a woman who exists and lives only for my dick.)

"Hmmmm, baby girl. How much would it cost for your own spot?"

Her eyes light up and she clasps her hand "A three bedroom in Baltimore shouldn't be more than 450. I could move in with you."

"Naw, baby girl, I like my space but if you can put it on me like you just did on a regular basis and cook for me like you just did I will pay for you a spot."

Her eyes go wide and she says "For real???"

"Hell yeah." in fact I hand her my card and tell her to go apartment hunting today and "Let daddy know what you find".

"But you can't slack off. You take care of my needs and I will take care of yours."

She promises, "Daddy, I will make you so happy you won't believe. Just give me the chance." She seems to be on the verge of tears and I smile.

"Call me or text my cell today when you find something."

"Ok boo." She smiles and says "Of course and just for that, I got a good morning surprise." She drops to her knees and thanks me the best way she knows how. By the time she finishes my legs are trembling in involuntary spasms, and I can't believe she ate the whole thing. Damn.

She hops up grabs her clothes and stashes them in her bags and says, "Talk to you soon daddy."

I'm groggy but damn I feel good.

CHAPTER 6

Back into the Grinder

MY ALARM GOES OFF again at 8:30. Shit I'm gonna be late to court. I quickly get to my feet. I throw on my olive Brooks Brother suit. It came straight from the outlet store. This means it will last me less than a year. With my brown Kenneth Cole shoes on, I walk out my door. The same two Asian coeds walk by me smiling. This time I'm so tired from Trina. I ignore them. I could have sworn I felt one of their hands traipsed across my backside. I quickly turn and look at them but they seem to be deep in conversation. I turn back to my door. After I finish locking my door, I turn back and look again. I could swear that the tallest one does a slow wink at me then turns her attention back to her friend. I guess that screaming from Trina last night got that girl's attention. I guess if she had never heard Trina's screams of pleasure she would have never looked at me. But now that she heard them she wants to know me. She wants to know what's up. She wants to know if I can play her strings like I played Trina's last night. But the last thing on my mind is sex. I glance at my black Skagen watch and the time is 8:39 AM. I need to be in court by nine so I attack the stairs and briskly walk the fifteen minute walk to the courthouse. As I walk, I get a text message from Trina which is a pic of her in her birthday suit and the message "thank you daddy" written across the bottom. Wow this is gonna get a brotha some fun. I figure that for 450 a month Pocahontas' pussy is a small price to pay. Then looking at my phone I see I have a missed call and a voice mail message. Oh shit Carmen called last night. I quickly check the voicemail. Carmen's sweet voice coos at me. "I tried to catch you leaving the courthouse last night. I was trying to catch you but when I saw you make a left on Baltimore St.

I lost sight of you. You weren't on the Block last night, were you naughty boy???? Call me." I gulp so loudly that a passerby looks at me in amusement. Shit don't tell me I lost a woman who could be my dream because I couldn't control my cock again. I have flashbacks to the last fight with my wife with her crying and sobbing. I stood there watching her with guilt in my eyes. I had another woman's perfume on my body and her secret scent on my cock. Pussy aroma seeped through all of it. It was not a good day. What the hell am I gonna do? I could love Carmen but I can fuck Trina any which way I want when I want how I want and it felt good. What the fuck should I do? I know of course. What I need to do is forget about my dick and concentrate on Billy Badass' trial before he ends up on death row. Should he end up on death row because I couldn't fucking concentrate? I take a deep breath and grab the door to the courthouse. I walk in. I flash my attorney's green card and continue in. I take the steps two at a time and walk into the judge's courtroom with three minutes to spare. I open my brief case and set down my laptop and papers. Just as corrections brought my client into the courtroom, I sat down.

Billy looks like he has aged ten years in the last few days. His eyes have hollowed out. His muscular arms have atrophied and look weak. His cheeks look slack. There seems to be a new patch of grey hair emerging from the front of his head. Wow, maybe he has learned his lesson. Maybe now he will fly the straight and narrow from now on. Yeah right! Wishful thinking. That brings to mind a different defendant, a killer I cross-examined in federal court in Brooklyn years ago. He was directly responsible for around twenty deaths. He had the audacity during cross examination to tell me and the jury that no matter that even though he had killed twenty people, the three years he had spent in jail had reformed him. He would never be a menace to society ever again. If he was let out right now, he would be a changed man. It's amazing what your choices in life can do to you. Look at me I was driven from my home and spent my night in the arms of a stripper instead of the arms of my family. Choices suck. I guess it would be like me promising my wife

"I know you divorced me but now that I have spent time as a lonely single man, I will never again cheat or stray from your side. I'm a changed man." Yeah, like she would believe that. I didn't even believe that myself. But I digress.

Billy sits down and holds his head in his hands and asks, "Mr. Davis, What's gonna happen today?" "Well, I believe that the case detective is going to testify today." The case detective just happens to be my homey Head. Head and I are close friends. It seemed logical that it was time for him to testify. This logical assumption held out until Lok stood up and called his chief CSI Guy John Beebe. I call him John B. He is a 57 year old pocket-protector wearing investigator. He has thick black glasses with tape in the middle. He is a genius investigator who is much better than the City of Baltimore deserves but he has his dark side and a preference for chickenheads. Those hood rat sistahs. That makes him Baltimore for life even though he is a double Johns Hopkins grad and had been offered jobs in Miami, Florida and Orange County, California. Baltimore has more hood rats per square inch than any city in America except in Brooklyn and John B. hates the cold of New York, so I guess its Baltimore's finest gain.

John Beebe walks in from the back of the courtroom. He is wearing his white lab coat, his glasses, and the aforementioned pocket protector. He has on nondescript tan pants and a picnic tablecloth checkered shirt. Looking exactly like what he is. I look in the back corner and there is Mr. GrayBoy still looking like the pimp and low life he is. He is sitting on the defense side of the courtroom. If the jury thinks that scumbag is in support of my client, that's another strike against him. John Beebe takes the stand. I ask Judge P. if I can approach. The judge crinkles his face at me and looks irritated. He motions me and Lok forward and with a brusque "What is it now counsel?" he directs me to speak. I give a stage whisper that I'm sure the jury could hear "Your honor, that gigolo that is sitting behind my client has nothing to do with my client and it may give the jury the impression that he is with my client and he isn't." Lok shrugs his shoulders and says it's a free country. The judge barks, "Mr. Davis.

Courtrooms are open to the public so whether that pimp looking cracker is not with you, I can't control where he sits." The judge's tone is as loud as my "stage whisper" so while denying my request to kick GrayBoy out, the judge and I have made it clear to the jury that he isn't with us. GrayBoy glares at me as I walk back to the table. Glaring is all he will do. He knows I know too much about where his bodies are buried literally because I have represented him before on a shooting on the west side. His defense was he couldn't have committed the shooting because was committing a murder on the east side at the same time. I managed to convince him that it wasn't a really good defense to admit to a capital crime to beat a lesser felony. The jury kicked the case because one of GrayBoy' girls got on the stand and admitted the shooting and did his time for him.

As I take my seat Lok starts questioning John B. John B. has a squeaky high voice that changes to a Barry White after four or five shots of Hennessy. He comes off as the brilliant professor who is a little absent minded. You forgive him because he is so smart that he can be dumb sometimes. John reviews the evidence. A fingerprint that matches my client was found on the inside of the victim's car on the steering wheel and on the seatbelt latch on the driver's side. John explains how the fingerprints have 12 points of comparison that match. Points of comparison are simply defined grooves or swirls in a fingerprint that can be matched from the found print to the known patterns of a subject's hands which makes the chances astronomical that they came from anyone else. Billy was a man who was just as certain to have touched the items as he was certain as to have touched Laquaana upside her head when she didn't listen to him. Billy touched the items. But the beauty of fingerprints is that they only tell you that someone touched an item but not when that touch happened. That is the rub with the technology. It is a certain identifier as to the identity of who touched it but not when. That gives a shark like me the wiggle room that I need to cast doubt on rock solid evidence. "Ain't life grand?" My job is to turn what is irrefutable to what is irreputable. No wonder, I'm disgusted with my practice and my career so much. John B drones on about the differences between grooves and swirls, about distinct points of comparison. Even though he initially did an eyeball comparison, he went on to more accurately confirm it when he ran the prints though AFI (the Automated Fingerprint Identification System more commonly called AFIS). After running the prints through AFIS, guess whose fingerprints matched? Billy Badass. I didn't panic or wet my pants, unlike Billy Badass who emitted a smell reminisce of hot garbage mixed with old cheese and body odor. It's one of the unknown truths of trial work. When a point hits home, client's bowels tend to loosen and they admit a smell that probably should be classified as "got damn he's guilty". The guys can control their facial twitches, their eyes and body language, but I have yet to meet the criminal who can control the smell that emits when the prosecution scores with a real dead on point. I try to softly gasp for air without seeming to gag. I turn away from the trial table and pretend to rifle through my brief case as if I'm going to pull out the piece of evidence that is gonna blow this case open. But the reality is that a nigga needs to breathe. I take gulps of air that clear my lungs and I refrain from scowling at my client so I won't hurt him in front of the jury. Lok Yao starts to wind down with John B when he says "Can you, to a reasonable degree of scientific certainty, tell how unlikely it would be that those fingerprints come from someone else?" With a pregnant over-dramatic pause John B looks down, shuffles his notes, looks up, pushes his black plastic glasses back up from the tip of his nose and states "I can". Yao says, what is that likely? John says it's scientifically impossible. The odds are greater than the number of people who exist on earth. The certainty is greater that these fingerprints belong to Mr. Johnson than to any human being who has ever lived. There's a deep rumble from the audience but the jury remains stone-faced and as inscrutable as Buddha.

Yao looks up and tells the judge "Your honor, I believe that this would be a good stopping point for the day. The next witness will be a little longer." I immediately stand up and say "Your honor I know it's 4:15, but since Mr. Lok is finished, my cross won't be long." The judge gives his assent by nodding his head and Lok stares daggers at me. I smirk at him and proceed to ask John about his background and history carefully avoiding our joint whore mongering. I do know that John was fired from his first job as a medical examiner in Tuscaloosa, Alabama for alleged incompetence. Actually he got caught fucking the chief examiner's college- age chocolate deluxe daughter in a morgue drawer. I can't help it if some things are just below the belt in more ways than one. Believe it or not, attorneys and court personnel know more about each other than they should. If we let the cat out of the bag, in every trial there will be no one left to practice law or administer justice. I proceed to drill John B. about his background. This continues for about fifteen minutes and Judge smirks at me and says "Mr. Davis, we will stop there for the day," and dismisses the jury for the day. I then ask the judge to admonish John that he is now under cross-examination and to have no conversation with the prosecution. See this is why Lok is fuming. At this point, he can't consult with his chief scientific witness overnight about the case and any findings, because he is now subject to cross-examination and therefore barred from talking to him about the case. This is just one of my dirty little tricks in the defense attorney's handbag that can be used to needle the opposing counsel without giving the appearance of being discourteous. It's not like the judge, counsel, the court officers, and anyone else who has spent five minutes in a courtroom don't know why I did this. It's just that Lok can't prove it and I get to throw a road block in his way. I pack up my bag and turn to Billy whose current smell is giving new meaning to the term Badass. I say, "Smell you later," and I pushed through the low swinging doors that divide that bar from the audience. I walk to the door towards freedom, fresh air, and my steady piece of ass that is waiting for me in my office. My secretary gives the best head in the world and, right now, that's what I need.

CHAPTER 7

Alone with My Conscience

CRIMINAL LAW IS LIKE a sewer - black insipid poison that seeps inside you. It poisons your humanity. Other people see parks where children play and flowers grow. You see a crime scene where the only fruit is the strange fruit of a deceased human shell that Billy Holiday sang about.

That was in my mind as Christy in front of me reassembles her work outfit. She has just sucked me off to climax three times. I just love the image of a thick light skinned woman with blondish hair on her knees in front of me sucking my cock. The mere thought of that makes me as hard as Chinese arithmetic but the reality of it is even better. She smiles at me as she saunters back to her desk where she picks up her Chanel bag, courtesy of her grateful boss. She walks toward the door where she is on her way to meet her preacher husband. Wow!

You would think all this sex would put me in a better mood. It does temporarily but I slip into a black mood when I consider the mess I've made of my life. Heck, I never ever bought my ex-wife a Chanel bag. I'm a scum bag. I hate my job of fighting for scum-bags. I hate the women who give me sexual gratification because they are inadequate to my needs -not my sexual needs but my companionship needs. I know intuitively that not one of them would have been around if I was broke and not a lawyer. They gravitated into my orbit not because of their love or desire for me but their desire to be near someone successful. They want success to rub off to them in the form of cars, Chanel bags, jewelry, and cash money. I just use that sex to keep from feeling so alone. I use sex to rage against the darkness in my mind. My sex addiction seems to make me slip in even deeper into the black morass of moral uncertainty and depression. When I say moral uncertainty I am only fooling myself. I know my moral uncertainty is moral depravity. I know it as sure as I know that sex is only a salve and not my salvation. As I sit there morosely with my head on my desk, I hear a knock at the outer door of my office and in walks my Carmen. She has on a dark green Jones of New York business suit with a short skirt that cuts at mid-thigh and shows the curves of her legs so perfectly that it's as if they were carved from marble. If I could have this woman in my life she could be my salvation because right now I definitely need saving. I have become a lawyer named Jasper instead of Jasper who happens to be a lawyer. It has seeped into and corrupted every part of my life. I'm lost. The nastiness I employ in work has become the manner in which I deal with everyone in my life. The angles I look for in trial to help my clients and get over on an unsuspecting jury are the angles that I employ in my life to get over on the people in it as well. The cocksure arrogance that I show the jury has replaced the love I used to project to those I care about. I'm a facsimile of who I used to be and it damn sure ain't reasonable. I'm hoping that by reaching out to this angel I can become something of a reasonable approximation of my former self. Maybe Carmen can save me. All this passes through my mind while I stare and give Carmen a plastic smile and hello. The only genuine feeling that I have at that point is despair and a prayerful hope that this beauty is my angel savior and grantor of the grace I so sorely need. I rise from my desk and hug her. The light scent of her J. Lo perfume fills my nostrils and warms me and makes my manhood tingle. I have a quick mental flash of her skirt bunched around her waist as she is bent over my desk. I imagine myself entering her from behind while she moans with her arms reached out to grasp the far edge of my desk as she moans my name. I visibly shake my head and push that thought out of my head. This is my angel, my savior and she is not to be treated like all the whores who have been in my life. She is my muse and she must be put on a pedestal. My sexual desires would corrupt her and doom me to a life in the hell I am currently in.

They are not a way to salvation. She smiles and says, "Hey, where were you last night? I wanted to spend time with you. I saw your car and knocked at your door but there was no answer. Where were you?" Carmen looks at me from behind her tortoise shell glasses and wrinkles her cute cinnamon colored nose and stares at me with just a slightly accusatory glance." I went over to John's apartment on the fifth floor and we watched the Wizards' game and drank beer until late.... What time did you come by?" knowing all the while the knocks that came at my door at 6:30.... She says "Oh yeah, right, the tip off was at 7:00. I was gonna surprise you with tickets to the game. We could have gone together. I had to go with my girlfriend Migdia and she is wild. She kept passing notes to the players on the bench all game and then she dragged me to the after party at the bar in their hotel and all I wanted to do was be with you. I wish you had been with me." I take the gulp of the unrepentant and say a silent "shit." Instead of being with a Goddess I was with a whore. How fucking stupid am I? A LAWYER WHO LOVES SPORTS and all she wanted to do was take me to see my favorite sports team and hold my hand all night that. Well I guess when you do shit, you get shit back in the end and this was my just desserts. I mumble my apology and Carmen goes off to talk about how good I was in trial today. I didn't even notice her in there. I guess I was so preoccupied with or, in the alternative, bored with my trial so I didn't even glance around and notice my angel. I asked her what part did she like the best. She said, "The part when you stranded John on the stand knowing the prosecutor can't talk to him." "So, you saw that huh? My respect for this great woman is growing. I say, "Where can I take you to dine tonight?" "Nowhere. I have to go to work tonight back at the club", she said. Shit I lost out on my chance to be in heaven for a quicky fuck in hell. Shit. Shit! Carmen says "I just wanted to see you, Jasper, today and let you know you're on my mind and that you're in my spirit" I immediately envision Carmen's beautiful golden aura with a dark blood red black spot that represents my corrupting influence in her life. Now I feel like an idiot. I'm a corrupt asshole. How much more can a motherfucker bear?

Carmen looks at me, smiles over the tops of her glasses, and kisses me with her full lips. Her tongue runs over my lips not in my mouth just the surface giving me a small taste of her flavor but not enough to quench my thirst for her essence. "I gotta go. Bye bye." she says and turns to leave but I refuse to let her go... "Jasper. I gotta go to work. Let go." she smiles and her dimples are showing. I said, "Letting you go is the one thing in my life I am no longer capable of doing. I could easier give up breathing and eating than I could give up your scent, your smile, and your presence in my life." She smiles and pulls her fingers loose of my hand and flounces to the door. I am mesmerized by her perfect cheerleader's pout butt. I am mesmerized by her whole being. I stand there for a full five seconds after she closes the door and I can't move because I feel like my life has just walked out of the door. It has been a long time since I felt like this. I didn't think a woman could mesmerize me with her presence anymore. I thought I was immune through the vaccination of divorce. I would have never guessed that I could feel like this again. I'm immediately scared because I know that a woman like that can take control of my senses, my being, my whole life without hardly even trying. That shit fucks with me. I collapse back in my chair and roll back and forth in my chair going 7 inches forward and 7 inches back each time. Am I in trouble? I gotta get out of here and get my control back. Get a grip, JD. I've got to get control. I grab my brown leather brief case and shove God knows what papers in there. Man, I don't know what I'm doing. I loosen my tie and stagger to the elevator. As I wait I see my face reflected in the shiny gold doors of the elevators. I am staring at a face I just don't recognize. I mean, I see my eyes, my suit, my goatee and my shiny bald head and my black metal glasses but I don't recognize the spirit in the face. Who am I? I'm not the joyful playful man I have spent my life as. I see an old soul full of weariness and maybe just a touch not of playfulness but of evil. Real evil. I start feeling sad and as my face droops in sadness, the glint of evil sparks like a white hot fire. Just then the elevator bell rings and the door opens and there is the most gorgeous snow bunny in that elevator. Her name is

Sunny and she's a receptionist for Dewey Cheatem and Howe. Dewey Cheatem and Howe is my pet name for the civil litigation firm on the top floor of the building. Sunny is a California surfer girl who relocated to Maryland for school. She realized two things: 1. School wasn't quite for her and 2. There are advantages to being the only trim athletic blonde 38C California girl in a particular time zone. It had paid off for Sunny to the tune of $75K a year and a Corvette convertible and loft apartment in the harbor all courtesy of the here boss Robbie Howe, an 89 year old leech who probably couldn't tap that ass if he wanted to ,but gets the pleasure of looking at Sunny all day. I know all this because she and Christy, my secretary, are buddies and thick as thieves. Christy is hinting for me to do some of the same things for her. I guess she keeps forgetting that she is married. Her husband would wonder where all that stuff came from. Plus, the fact is, I'm a cheap bastard. Sunny smiles and says "Good evening, Mr. Davis. Oh poor baby, you look so worn out. Are you leaving?" I nod my head weakly and slump against the back of the elevator, the perfect position to observe Sunny's posterior as the elevator descends. I wonder how many asses can I stare at before I become an ass. Is this what my life has become? Fighting for criminals and chasing ass? Man this is depressing just as I'm about to drown in my self-pity, the elevator bell rings as we reach the ground floor. Sunny turns around waves and smiles and says, "Goodnight, Mr. Davis", and wiggles out of the elevator. I sling my briefcase over my left shoulder and dangle my suit coat off of my fingertips of my left hand and let it fall over my back. I start my five minute walk to my apartment. As I walk up Baltimore Street, I see two hood rats with fat butts and jeans so tight that I can read their minds. They are oblivious to me. I sigh and trudge on. I see a line of teenagers and twenty somethings at the Mariner Arena which is diagonal from my building. I look up and read the marquee and see that young something and lil' somebody are performing there tonight. Oh well, there goes a quiet night. There will be college kids everywhere tonight around the complex. This is good because I get to look at sexy girls, but bad because that means the attendant thugs, drug dealers and noise pollution that follow those nubiles will be there too. I decided that tonight I'm gonna grab some KFC a block away and stay in and watch repeats of Dexter on tv. I take a right on Howard Street and walk one block past my apartment to KFC. Like every other restaurant and every inch of the neighborhood it is swarmed with the hood rats and thugs that were around the Mariner Arena. I wait in line for 15 minutes until I reach the front. An older woman with a gap tooth smile and a few rotten teeth takes my order. She smiles at me and takes my money. She gives me my change. She hands me my 12-piece bucket of spicy chicken. I walk down one block and pick up a pint of my namesake Mr. JACK DANIELS. I walk into my building and trudge up the stairs. I turn my key in my lock. I close the door; drop my jacket and briefcase on the floor at the door. I take the chicken and the Jack and walk over to my 55 inch projection TV. This TV was the only thing I got in the divorce besides my soul and BMW. My wife got a lien on that too. I turn it on with a press of a button. The remote has never been present in my life. I flop down in my easy chair and check the DirecTV guide on screen and pick out the latest Dexter that has been recorded and I take a deep swig of the whiskey. My throat burns assuring me I'm still alive. Jack Daniels just confirmed that.

The alcohol can't burn a dead man so "I drink therefore I am". As I sit there my thoughts drift back to a retrospective of my last five years of life. As I sit, there I notice a spot of chicken on my black Brooks Brother suit that I have worn the last three days in row. A tear drops out of my eye. Since I lost my family I just don't take care of myself. It is as if I had no pride. It is as if I have no respect for myself. Pride doesn't make you dress neat and clean, respect does. In fact my pride wouldn't let me acknowledge how I neglected my attire, my health and general well-being. If I could respect myself, I would. But I can't. How can I respect a whore-monger who is trying to squeeze a psychopathic killer through the slit of reasonable doubt to keep him from meeting the justice he richly deserves? How can I respect myself when I constantly fantasize and indulge in sex all the freaking time? How can I even find the time to practice law? How do I find time to live with my pulse driven dick. I can't breathe if I can't feel if I can't be human again and not a six foot walking talking hard-on with a drinking problem.

I feel myself drifting off to sleep. I snap awake jerking my head forward and I drop my bucket of chicken and the Jack Daniels falls to the floor with a noticeable clink. I look at it, still sealed, no leak so it's good to go. I struggle to an upright position. I glance at the clock. It's 3:02 am and the TV is still on with a blaring infomercial. Infomercials are there enough to make you wish that TV channels would have the decency to go off the air this late at night like they used to when I was a kid. Nowadays anything is done to make a buck including overloading our senses with ads and sales and bullshit that we don't need and stuff that kills us. I pick up the chicken off the floor. It's past the five second rule but fuck it. I open the Jack, take a swallow and let the burn relax me. Setting the Jack Daniels on the counter, I crawl into my unmade bed and pull my comforter on top of me. I set my alarm and for the first time in a while I go to bed by myself. Damn it feels good. I reach over and turn on my fan so I can have a cool breeze on my face and slowly I close my eyes and fall asleep with a smile on my face.

CHAPTER 8

Testimony Day-Lead Detective

MY ALARM GOES OFF with a blare and I sit up straight with a start. I glance at the clock. It's 7:30. I groan and slam my head back down to my mattress. I guess I must have slid back some because I missed the mattresses. I slammed the back of my head directly onto headboard of my IKEA futon. I see stars and an explosion bursts before my eyes. I yelp in pain, grab the back of my head and I lean toward putting my face toward my lap. SHIT I GOTTA GET MY BLACK ASS UP AND IN COURT. I hate it when I wake up late. Unfortunately for me, alcohol will overcome and silence any alarm clock. It has the ability to make me deaf to alarm clocks. I groan. I swing my feet over the edge of the bed and wobbly rise to my feet. Lances of pain shoot through my basketball-addled knees as I drag myself toward the bathroom. I place my hands and face on the cool slate tile of the bathroom counter. I put my finger down my throat. It feels so good. Wow, when I was in college my face would have had to be against the pissy tile floor for this type of relief (I guess I'm moving up in the world). I slowly open one eye and peek at myself. Sheeeeyyyyyiit I'm a fucking mess. I open both eyes and take myself in. There are pieces of fried chicken and what seems to be throw up on my shirt, my suit pants, and on my chest. It looks like a mix of chewed up chicken and Kool-Aid. I don't even remember drinking Kool-Aid. I guess I just lost control and must have done stuff while my conscious mind was shut off. This sucks. I stretch and yawn and as I stretch I catch a charley-horse in the back of my right leg. The pain is so intense it feels like the contracting muscles are trying to break the bones of my legs. I slump to the floor and grab my leg. I grimace and drag myself over to the tub and run the hot water. Stripped of my ruined suit pants and food speckled dress shirt, I drop my ass into the hot water. Ah, instant relief as I lay my head back as the jacuzzi jets kick on. I exhale loudly and groan, finally bliss. I'm going to be late for court but some things are worth it. After 20 minutes of soaking, I feel somewhat restored. The thump in my head has softened to a dull roar. I stand up and let the water drop off my skin. I walk into the main part of my loft apartment. I prefer drip dry to towels. I grab the Vaseline and oil up my dry ass skin. I run over to my luxurious collection of Wal-Mart suits. I select a tan suit with a blue shirt. Since orange is my favorite color, I select the orange tie. I glance at my clock and realize that I'm not going to be late after all.

What a miracle of miracles! It's 8:30 AM. I can still make it to court on time. I slip on my leather Stacey Adams trial boots. I grab my briefcase and head to the door. I sling my briefcase over my back and turn to close my door. And the same two Asian girl neighbors come walking by. They are smiling and giggling. The taller one hands me a note. She smiles and they lean into each other as they walk quickly away giggling and looking back. I watch their young tight buns twitch as they walk away from me. I look at the note. It's on parchment paper. On the front there appears to be one red lipstick kiss and one purple lipstick kiss. The same color lipstick that they each seem to have on each time I see them. The note reads you make so much noise every night that we have trouble sleeping, especially when you have your female company singing to orgasms. That usually helps us sleep but last night it was so quiet that we both got frustrated and decided that maybe tonight you can help sing us to sleep as well. I sag against the door I can't believe it. Man, this day is going to seem like it takes a year to get through the trial, nigga. I got a threesome with two Asian college chicks waiting on me? How the fuck am I going to concentrate on trial when my little head is focused on freaking. The reality is I do it every day I focus on trial while my dick thinks about sex.

I remember the trial in New York when over the lunch break I fucked the court reporter over her desk ten feet from the courtroom. And then went back and got my scumbag client acquitted of two counts of rape of two teenage girls. The defense was consent and that they cried rape after my client spread the news over the neighborhood and posted the video on the Internet. He was a first class asshole, but not a rapist, but I'm sure the year he spent in jail awaiting trial will make him a much nicer gentleman and more courteous to the ladies. Yeah right. I walk briskly to the front door; I hail a cab. I just don't feel like walking anymore today. I hop into a hack. A hack is a Baltimore gypsy cab where people who are driving along stop and pick up people to make a few extra bucks with no taxi license. My taxi is a red, two door Honda Accord. He zooms down Baltimore Street and busts the left to take me to the Clarence Mitchell Courthouse. I pay him seven bucks. I walk into the courthouse. I'm so early the courtrooms are still locked. I take a can of Coke, my early morning picker upper, out of my bag. I sit down on the marble bench outside the courtroom. I pull an airplane bottle of Jack Daniels out and empty it into the can.

I pull the Baltimore City Paper out of my bag and read the headlines. I first drag my eyes to the small box called Murder Ink. This column keeps the weekly murder count in Baltimore. The murder count is 265 murders in Bodymore Murdaland as of this week. Business is booming. The whole rest of the country is in a recession but the criminal prison industrial complex is in a boom as the economy gets bad fringe people are dragged into a life of crime because they have to support their families and themselves. If people think Reaganomics was bad, it was nothing compared to what W did to the country but I digress. A sheriff's deputy pokes his head out of the courtroom and says" Counsel, we are now open." I fold the paper and swallow down the rest of my Coke. I stand up and burp. I walk in the courtroom. In walks Billy, in chains and shackles doing the inmate shuffle on the way to the trial table. Apparently, Yao entered through the back of the courtroom. He's already set up and twirls in his chair (well they always give prosecutors any breaks they can) I great him with a grunt. Today is the day Head gets on the stand and I'm going to have to tear my drinking buddy a new asshole for Billy to have a chance of even getting a hung jury. The judge comes into the room not in his robe but in a white oxford and slacks. Everyone jumps to their feet and he waves us down. "No not yet, be at ease" he says. He sits down on the bench peers over his glasses and starts pecking away at his keyboard. I get set, lay out my notebooks, power up my Dell, and plug myself into my iPod, so I can get myself ready for the clash. I put on my hype songs in order: Ice Cube "It was a good day," DMX "They Don't Know," and Arrested Development, "Everyday People." After Speech says, "Act like a nigga and get stomped by an African", I'm good to go. I'm ready to kick some monkey ass specifically Head's monkey ass. An evil grin takes over my face.

My client looks at me. He notices the glare then asks "What the fuck is wrong with you?" I say, "Shut the fuck up I'm in the zone. If you want me to save your life you will sit the fuck down and shut the fuck up so I can handle your business, bitch." He's so taken aback by what I say and how I say it that he physically rears back. With a surprise look all over his face, body, and spirit he looks like, "What the fuck? This nigga ain't no joke." I turn away from him and I turn around, and I focus for the next fifteen minutes on the witness chair. My focus doesn't wave as the bailiff/deputy calls court to order. My focus doesn't waver as the jury walks in. I can feel my glands salivating as Head takes the witness stand he looks at me and smiles, but I can tell he is unnerved by me because he keeps glancing back at me. I never blink. I never move my head or smile. I just keep staring. Lok looks at me curiously. He's never seen me like this before. But Head has. He keeps glancing over at me. He's sweating bullets like a preacher in a whorehouse. He keeps looking over me as if to say "Motherfucker what you doing? It's me, Head, nigga, your boy." I see Sadie, the courtroom clerk whose almost as experienced as the judge giggle. She's seen me like this before and she knows it's on. After the jury slowly files in, Lok slowly but cautiously begins his cross-examination of his lead detective in this murder, Head. Lok takes Head thru his call out to the scene, his first impressions of the scene the position of the body and who was there when he got to the scene when he arrived there. He describes the body already in rigor and the blood pooled beneath the body in a depression in the concrete beneath it. He talked about the victim's 25 year old girlfriend whose white dress was turned red by the victim's blood. She had been draped over the body crying when the first officer arrived at the scene. Head then pointed out the high yellow with the pixie haircut sitting behind the bar on the prosecution table. He identified her as Roxanne, the same woman who was on the scene covered by blood. At just that moment tears start streaming down Roxanne's face. (Just wait till I show the pictures I have of her to the jury.) Yao pulls out a full color blowup of the victim's body at the scene with a harsh bright police light shining on the body. This is the type of scene you might see at a slasher film. I see a few women on the jury visibly gasp when they see the body lying in situ. Head id's the picture and then glances over at me. Beads of perspiration are running rivulets down his face.

He id's the picture and confirms that's what he saw on the scene when he arrived. He then explains that when he got the physical evidence, there were the fingerprints of Billy Badass taken from the car and from the ignition key that was found in the dead man's pocket. He further elaborates that this match was made by a computer database known as AFIS (which to the uninitiated means automated fingerprint identification system.... Billy's fingerprints are in there for his prior criminal convictions). I object to this because under the rules of evidence he hasn't testified his prior criminal convictions are not properly introduced at this point. The judge sustains my objections and directs the jury to disregard the statement. Judge P. also excuses the jury for its midmorning break. When they leave the room he proceeds to ream Head and Yao a new asshole for getting into Billy's prior convictions. He leaves the bench with this warning. "If you let this happen again, Detective and Mr. Lok. I will have both your badges hanging on my mantelpiece as trophies. This is a murder case and if you continue to F-up, you will lose this case and I will string you up. Detective you will be answering to the police chief and Mr. Lok you will be answering to the bar! Do I make myself clear?" Clearly contrite they both say yes and Judge P. slams his trial book closed and stomps out of the courtroom. The bailiff announces that his court will be in recess for the next 15 minutes. I slide on my silver iPod Nano and I start listening to the Fat Boys, "Can you feel It" followed by MC Hammer, "Turn this Mother Out" and ending with TI's "Dead and Gone." By that time the judge comes back, Head is back on the stand and the jury is back in the box. Head is much worse for the wear. The judge's reaming and my stare has really unnerved him. I can clearly see the wet sweat stains on the underarms of his suit jacket. He has sweated all the way through his suit jacket even though the courtroom is an even 65 degrees. Thing is, I don't remove my glare but I quickly mouth the word "boo!" and I see Head jump a few inches in the air in reaction. He's my bitch and ready to be bent over. He looks at me with a pleading look. "Jasper I'm your boy, don't do it." Lok picks up from where he left off.

Head relates how he received tips from three of his snitches as to what occurred. As soon as he says "They told me." I am up and objecting. Judge P. sustains and glares first at Yao and then Head. You can tell the judge is ready to blow a gasket. Yao clears his throat and says, "Detective, without telling us what they said, what did you do as a result of your conversations with these three informants? What did you do?" "I immediately got warrants for the arrest of one William Johnson a.k.a. Billy Badass." And Yao asks, "Do you see Billy Badass in court here today." "Yes I do. He's sitting at the defense table with the shaved head and goatee and the white shirt." Yao asks for the judge to note the identification. I object because I also have a shaved head, goatee, and white shirt on under my suit jacket. Judge P. smirks and sustains my objection. Head further adds "He's the bigger one with the 4 inch knife scar under his left eye." I give up and the judge notes the in-court id and then its lunch time. At lunch, I go down to the Norma Jean's bar. With my two beer lunch, I get three lap dances with two different honeys. "Oh all that beautiful black love!!!!" On the way back to the courthouse, I stop at the nearby Seven Eleven and get some Altoids breath mints.

Can't let the client smell the beer on my breath. I also take the spray can of Right Guard I keep in my briefcase and spray my suit so I don't smell like the smoky ass bar I just left. At least, I didn't have to worry about cum stains. I guess my underwear soaked up the nut that the thick light-skinned girl grinded out of me at the last lap dance. I guess my underwear caught that. Today was the first in a while that I wasn't free balling. As I walked up Baltimore Street I caught a glance of myself. As I walked by one of the bright shiny buildings with reflective glass, I catch a look at myself. I almost didn't recognize myself. I saw the three day growth of a beard. I saw the worn down suit, the shirt with food stains, and I was almost floored by my appearance. I can't recognize myself as the classy litigator who fought for the Constitution nor as the loving dad who was always there for his child. I'm just a facsimile of what I used to be. I'm depressed. I continue on the way to the courthouse. As I walk in I see everyone gathering I try to get my game face back on, but it just won't come back.

There is something missing. Head is looking at me with a puzzled expression on his face. He can see something is different. I just can't get my focus; I feel worn down. I look awful. As the jury files in, the judge reconvenes the case. Head details the arrest take down of Billy and the procedure of processing him into the system. He details the inventories of items in his pockets. He also details the clothes he took from him that had what appeared to be bloodstains on his dark blue jeans. He discusses how they were collected and sent to the lab. After the jeans are introduced, Yao is finished with Head. I get up and stride to the lectern to begin my cross exam. But as I walk up there, I feel like a relief pitcher who knows he doesn't have his fast ball that day. I start asking Head a few innocuous questions about the investigation and my voice is mild. I can't get my sarcastic tone back, it's just not there. I start asking Head about his informants and I start stuttering. I can't cleanly even ask a question. It's not that I'm drunk; I'm just not on the ball. If my trial work is usually a 100 percent, I'm at a 60- a failing grade. Not so bad that a jury that has never seen a criminal case would notice, but enough so I see the clerk frown and look at me because she has seen me at my best. I ask Head, "You rely on the words of felons and drug addicts to build your case against my client?" Head replies" Yes, of course. They are the people who inhabit your client's world, so they see what he does. No church folk or choirboys happen to be around when Billy is doing his thing.".... Head is looking at me quizzically. He can't figure out why I'm stumbling and bumbling... I try to pull it together. I say" Well all you have is the evidence that my client was in the car and touched the ignition key... I ask with a tone of disbelief. Head says in a measured tone, "Noooo. I have that plus the three eyewitnesses who told me they saw him do it. Plus I have blood found on his pants; plus I have the fact that he tried to run when we came to his house; plus we had his record of violence; plus his convictions of manslaughter prior to make him a prime suspect". I start yelling objection....

Judge P. slams his gavel down and looks at me evilly and says," Counsel you opened the door with the questions you just asked, now continue your cross or sit down, but don't you dare try those theatrics in my courtroom again". I stumble back to my seat and my client is seething.... "What the fuck was that? JD, are you trying to put me away? I paid you good money to defend me and you seem like your trying your best to get my ass a lethal injection..." I slump in my chair and say nothing. The judge decides that that is all for the day so at that point he dismisses the jury for the day and tells me he wants to see me in his chamber immediately. He tells Lok that this has nothing to do with the case and he will not be in the discussion. Lok starts to object but he decides that discretion is the better part of valor and says" Yes, your honor." As the deputies lead my angry client away and I slump in my chair and wallow in misery. No matter how much I debauched myself, I was always ready to answer the bell when it came to trial...today was the first day I realize that I'm not the lawyer I used to be. I accepted the fact that in my personal life I was a scumbag but I was still a scumbag that could defend criminals now I wasn't so sure anymore. Who am I if I can't try cases? I have never reached back for my fast ball and it wasn't there until now. The courtroom bailiff comes back into the courtroom and tells me that the judge is waiting on me in chambers and to get my ass in gear. I shove my notebook and laptop into my bag. I drag my body to the judge's chambers. He is sitting there with a pipe in his mouth looking at me the way an owl probably eyes a squirrel just before he swoops up and eats it." Mr. Davis, I've seen you fall a long way from the man you used to be. I never said anything because no matter how haggard you looked, when you came into my courtroom you could always perform in your client's best interest. What I saw today puts that into question. Look at you. You need a shave. That suit and shirt should be in the cleaners. You reek of Right Guard mixed with beer and smoke. I won't tell you how many times deputies or other attorneys have seen you come from the block in the middle of the day but now it's becoming a real problem. I'm going to be watching you very closely the rest of this trial. If I don't like what I see I'm going to have you removed from every criminal defense panel you serve on. I will bar you from my courtroom and report you to the bar." "Jasper", the judge says as he leans forward and reached his hand out to me, "Get yourself together. Get through this trial and get yourself together before you throw your life away. I've seen attorneys come and go. You were a star. Now I'm not sure who you are. Dry out. Get your game face back on and fight for you client." I mumble my thanks, sling my bag over my shoulder and make my way out of the office.

As I look back, I see Judge P. looking at me with a sad grandfatherly look on his face. That image stays with me the whole way as I trudge back to my condo. I drop my bag and sit in my lazy boy chair. I dropped my jacket to the floor, leant the chair back, and turned towards my window. I shove my hands in my pockets and stare into space for the next hour. I notice a piece of paper shoved in my pocket and I pull it out. It's the letter from the two Asian college-girls, my friendly neighbors, the China girls. I had forgotten they were coming over that evening. Here I am at the end of my rope losing my skills as a lawyer. I'm still thinking about meeting these girls instead of sobering up and refocusing. I debate this for another hour then I hear my door bell ring and who is it but the two beauties. One has a bottle of Jack in her hand and both are wearing overcoats hanging open to reveal the lingerie they both have on. "Hi, Jasper", they say in unison. I say hi and weakly I move out of their way and let them into the condo. They walk in shove me in my chair and take off their coats. "Jasper," says the shorter of the two, "We are gonna be your Courtesan girls tonight. If you don't know what that means, it means we are going to fulfill your every wish tonight and in return you are gonna fill us up with that monster you got in your pants," As the taller one grabs my cock thru my pants. Whew can a brotha catch his breath? For the next four hours they bathe me, feed me, massage me, and fuck me nonstop. By midnight, I feel like a horse that had been rode hard and put away wet. I think to myself as I fall asleep with one arm around each of the two little China girls. Hey maybe this is the way to get my mojo back. It's not the sex and liquor it's how I'm getting sex and liquor. If I can restrain myself to only a few women and drinks a few times a week I'll be able to pull myself together.

CHAPTER 9

Carmen's Dilemma

I AWAKE AT 6 O'CLOCK the next morning before my alarm even goes off. I actually feel refreshed. There is a note on the mirror in my bathroom. It reads: "We had a great time. Can't wait to see you again. We should make this a weekly thing." The letter is signed with two kisses one purple and one red. I stand at the toilet and take a piss that would make a racehorse jealous while I read the letter. I think maybe I have found my mojo. Is this the way I could run my life? It's not the fact that I'm drinking and fucking. It's the fact that I'm spreading it around way too much. Maybe Carmen and the courtesans are all I need. But then I'll need my secretary when I'm stressed out at work and maybe Pocahontas. Everybody needs chocolate every now and then. In my mind, I narrow myself down to 8 sex partners. It's interesting that I have included Carmen in this total when I have never had sex with her. I'm hopeful. At 6 o'clock sharp, I text her and ask if she has plans tomorrow. She texts right back "I'm not busy. Where are you going to take me?" She types a smiley face on the end. "How is the Hooters at the harbor?" I text back. She texts back "Ok big spender, I'll bite since FSU is playing Miami on TV tomorrow. See you at 7:30." OK cool, this is going to work. I need moderation in my life. I don't have to give up pussy. I just have to give up fucking everybody. I can do this. I don't have to fuck everybody.

I'm awake early. I feel refreshed and ready to confront the world. Just then I feel a throbbing in my front left temporal lobe (my brain), very sharp pain. Maybe I should replace the Jack Daniels with beer or at least replace it with beer three days a week; so, Jack four days, beer three days; that could work. I grab a Tylenol, grab my trial bag, sling it over my shoulder, and run to the door. This is going to be a great day. I'm going to beat Yao like he stole something from me. I look at my tan WalMart chic suit. It is fresh pressed. The shirt is a Brooks Brothers no iron but it looks like it needs a hit from an iron. As I bust a left out of my complex I see my two Asian honeys drive by in a red mustang convertible. They both wave, smile, and say, "Hey Jasper! See you later!" I yell back, "Hey ladies have a good day!" I rub my hand on my head and I notice I have a full week's growth. Now I started this trial with a clean-shaven head but now in the middle I have hair. That's not a good look. Well I'll take care of it before my date with Carmen tonight. I really don't care what the jury thinks of me only what my precious Carmen thinks. I start whistling on my way to the courthouse steps. I bound up the steps and stride confidently into the courtroom. As I start to set up my trial gear I notice that someone has placed an empty beer can with a napkin from Norma Jeans squarely in the middle of my trial table. I start to literally see red. How dare they! I never said anything when other lawyers got caught having sex with their clients in exchange for fees. I never disparaged Judge Godnow when his wife caught him as a male detention officer was giving him head in his office. And I certainly never said anything when the chief public defender got caught with 20 full-grown marijuana plants growing in her home. Yet these assholes decided that it would be fun to disparage me. That's ok. Nothing is going to throw me off my game. I crush the can. I throw it and the napkin into the garbage can under my wooden oak trial table. I hear snickers in the courtroom but I don't even raise my head up from my papers to see where it is coming from. They can't steal my dignity. I will not let them. By the time my client comes in, I'm sitting at the desk focusing on my laptop and my outline for the trial. I speak quietly to my client Billy as his shackles and chains are released. "Bill, we weren't hurt yesterday. Everyone they talked about will testify. Everything the detective said will be in front of this jury and will have less impact because the jury will expect it. "Billy looks at me like a little child looking at his dad.

This is surprising when his stare and sure size is taken into account. Billy says, "Mr. Davis you're all I got. I never had no family. My boys have taken over my business and my woman is warming Mr. GrayBoy bed at night. You're the only one who can give me back my life so I'm begging you to fight hard for me, sir." Right about then I get a whiff from his truth detector. I get a smell from his bowels. He is nervous, scared, and ready to cry. In fact, his eyes look swollen and red. I simply say, "I got you, Billy. I got you." As the jury files in and the judge takes the bench, I straighten my jacket and look at the jury. They are somber and poker faced. Out of the corner of my left eye I see Head staring at me grinning and shaking his head. He feels like he escaped unscathed. What he doesn't understand is that the points I scored won't be revealed until my summation. Then I will see if he still has that smile on his face. I know that Head must be the one who planted the beer and napkin because he is there as much as I am. In fact, his current sidepiece works there as a dancer. If he only knew that she is the one who gave me the lap dance that made me cum yesterday. What's the saying "It ain't no fun if the homies can't have none." After court is called to order, the judge instructs Yao to call his next witness. He promptly calls Markey Fortune. Markey is a big guy but he is wasting away from the inside. Heroin with a crack chaser will do that to you. Markey has a 52 page criminal history. Nothing more serious than armed robbery from twenty years ago before heroin got a hold of him at the age of 19. What was once a strong ambitious young hustler is now a shell of a 39 year old man who has seen life shit on him since he was a baby. Come on, Yao you have this fiend dressed up in a suit and tie? A jury will never look at him and see him as authentic. If they don't see him as authentic, how can they believe his story? So Markey stands up and affirms to tell the truth as a Muslim (he picked it up in prison) he will not swear. He settles into the chair and his basso sotto voice doesn't match his emaciated frame. He gives his name and address. Yao leads him through his history and criminal record to try and defuse the attack I would unleash on him if he didn't do so. He leads him directly to the incident so Markey says "We was all out there chillin' and Billy decided he wanted to drive the Monte Carlo with the ice cream paint job and the old boy said no." "By old boy you mean the victim, right?" Objection leading sustained rephrase... "Yeah that's who I mean."... Judge P. Judge P. turns to Markey, peers over his glasses at him and says, "Son, did you hear me say sustained?" That means you don't answer the question that is before you because I have ruled it improper. Understand?" Markey says, "Yeah." Judge P. Judge P. asks, "Does that mean Yes?" "Yes sir, Mr. Judge", Markey replies.

"Next question, Mr. Yao."

Yao says, "Who is 'old boy'?"

Markey replies, "The victim."

"Please continue."

"So Billy punches old boy in the face and takes his keys, gets in the car and starts the engine and listens to it purr. It sure sounded purty ... so he goes over to Linwood and says "Yo. I want your ride. How much?" By this time, Linwood is off the ground and his eye is swelling. He says, "It's not for sale I'm just waiting for my girl Roxanne to come out the building and I gotta have my ride. She actually owns it." I know everybody know that errand is picking up heroin and that girl ain't got no money to buy no car... old boy just don't wanna give up the ride.' Billy get mad and bitch slap him and says, 'Fuck you nigga.' Now old boy got some heart because he saw his girl coming out and walking towards him. So he says 'Fuck you too you bitch ass mark mutherfucker.' Well he shouldn't have done that. Billy came back and commenced to beating that ass, punching him in his face and when he fell to the ground, Billy started stomping him with his timberland in his face. Man I was 20 feet away and I heard old boy's skull crack from the stomping. Blood was pouring from his eyes, his nose and mouth. He pulled out a big silver gun and shot Linwood. Yo, there was blood everywhere. I was about to hurl, then Roxy ran over and grabbed Linwood and was yelling and crying and Billy over there just walked away. He hailed a hack (a hack is an unlicensed taxicab that can be driven by anybody with a car) and got the fuck, oh excuse me judge, I'm sorry, he got out of there fast. About 15 minutes later, the popo (police) arrived and then after another 10 minutes the ambulance arrived. But as soon as they got there, they put the white sheet over him because he was gone, man. That white sheet turned red from all that damn blood yo." Yao then asked, "Do you see the man who stomped on Linwood White's head in the courtroom today?" "Yes I do. He's that big ugly mug sitting with his lawyer JD... my man Jack Daniels." there is a nervous titter of laugher in the courtroom. I laugh slightly for being id'd in court by a fiend as Jack Daniels but I'm not going to object to the id because no one is going to mistake me for an ugly mug but Yao has to be a wiseass and says, "Which ugly mug do you mean?," with a smile on his face.

"I mean the bigger one," he replied and since Billy has me by 5 inches and 50 pounds, it's pretty easy to know who he means and the judge notes the in court identification of Billy. With that, Yao sits down and passes the witness to me.

I can feel Judge P.'s eyes boring into me. I can see Yao sitting back in his chair twirling his pen wondering if I'm going to repeat my fuck up of yesterday, I slowly coolly walk up to the podium. "Mr. Fortune, when you testified on direct you intimated that you knew me?"

"What you say JD? I ain't never been intimate with you. What you talking about?" Nervous laughter around the courtroom, I smile and laugh.

"Mr. Fortune, when I say 'intimated' I mean you implied you gave the impression that you knew me before today? Is that correct?"

Yao jumps up yelling, "objection."

Judge P. gruffly says "Sit down counsel. Your witness opened the door by calling defense counsel JD."

"Yeah, I know you man," drawled Markey. "You been representing me on and off with the po po for 15 years. Man, thanks again for getting me off on that murder charge. The police was crazy on that."

"You're welcome. Are there any other murders I got you off on besides that one?"

Judge P. growls, "Sustained. Move along counsel."

But the damage is done. I see the jury looking like they just ate something that tasted like ass. I then ask Markey, "Did you receive any offer or deal to testify today?" (for the uninitiated, in general, cooperating witnesses don't testify out of the goodness of their heart or out of a sense of civic duty. They do it because they get something: money, charges dropped, or a get out of jail free card.)

"Of course, son, you showed me the ropes back in 99. Yeah they gonna drop this little armed robbery situation that I got cause I'm testifying today."

I say, Thank you," and walk to my seat.

Markey yells, "yo JD, holla at me son. I know some ladies that want to meet you boy and some they got fat asses, boy." Judge P. gives Markey a withering look and he says "Oh, I'm sorry judge. I'm talking out of turn, right. Sorry. I just been in court so much I feel comfortable in this mutherfucker."

Judge P. holds his head in his hands and asks Yao if he has any more questions. He weakly answers, "No."

Judge P. tells the bailiff, "Get this person out of my damn courtroom."

I know Yao should be embarrassed about forgetting to put in Markey's record and deal before the jury before I got the chance to. I know I'm red faced by the idea of the jury thinking I would hang out with a creature like Markey but my mind also wanders and I wonder how fat those asses Markey was talking about are... as I daydream about 22 year old fat tight booties. I daydream through most of the testimony of the second snitch Elvira Jenkins a white poot boot female out of south Baltimore. She is a combination hooker booster and stickup artist. When she finds a john dumb enough or blind enough to want to fuck her. She is 36 but looks closer to 63 even through the pancake of makeup she has on to hide her pockmarked face.... Elvira is a DA's office official snitch.

Yao gets up and starts his direct of Elvira. He goes thru the preliminaries and then asks her "Ms. Jenkins, are you aware of the incident that has brought you to court today?" "Yes sir," answers Elvira.

Her black hair is pulled back in a bun and she is wearing a black wool sweater with a silk blouse whose collar pokes out through the neck of the sweater. She is doing her best schoolmarm impression and that might have worked if the jury hadn't seen the black micro mini shiny gold skirt she has on her bottom which also revealed the fuchsia silky thong she has on because it was so short. I guess when the DA's office dressed her top, they forgot her bottom. Trifling, it made me sick to look at that pockmarked booty as she walked in.

Elvira says "I was outside and I saw two black gentleman fighting... actually it seemed as if it wasn't really a fight but that big gentleman sitting right there (pointing directly at Billy) was beating an elderly man when I started seeing blood flying. Then I saw that man step on the head of the old man and I heard the sound of wood splitting or bone crunching and I saw blood shoot out of the old man's head like a geyser out of his eyes mouth and ears...I had to turn my head I couldn't stand to see that sight." Yao asks the judge to acknowledge the in court id of Billy... and I notice that Billy Butthole truth detector is acting again because this time the smell is like the rot that would be found in a defunct cheese factory in a barrel of Roquefort cheese that had sat for 20 years... sickening and wet.

"May I approach the witness?"

Judge P. says "Yes" and Yao approaches Elvira on the stand with the bloody picture of Linwood's body on display to everyone and Elvira sniffles and id's that as the man she saw beaten by Billy.

Yao asks her, "Have you been in trouble with the law before."

She says, "Yes I was a prostitute but I gave my life to Christ a while back and I haven't been the same since."...

"Did you get a deal for your testimony?"

"No."

Yao says, "No further questions."

Judge P. asks me if you want to start my cross-examination now or after lunch. I say, "After lunch is fine." I have my mind on doing the block crawl (for the uninitiated, the block crawl is going from one bar of the block to the next to the next until you have seen all the delights that all the bars have to offer then you go back to the one that has your favorite talent to watch and tip and get ridden by. So as Billy tries to ask me a question I snap my laptop shut ignoring his questions I walk quickly to the door of the courtroom as I reach in the door ... I take my Blackberry out and I text my investigator Norm Jones to follow Elvira after she leaves the courtroom to see what she does on her lunch break.

I start my pub-crawl at Norma Jean's seeing the sexy black girls but I think I need some white girl today after seeing Elvira I need some pancake butt rubbed on my Johnson. So I quickly head out, go back to the main block and commence to go in to the Double R Saloon. Inside, there are about three girls all looking like they have seen better days. They ask me where am I going as I head to the outdoor and I say, "I'm just looking around." I hear a chorus of "stay" but these bitches have seen better days so I head to the next bar Joey's. In Joey's, there are some young girls but the problem is that they seem too young. Either of these girls are fourteen or they are on a straight heroin diet and that has eaten at all the fat of their body. They really look like they are children but the hollowed out eyes tell the tale of their heroin addiction. I immediately do a u-turn as soon as it registers. These girls are too zoned out to even respond to me leaving... Next I head into Passion there is a thick red head white honey with a tramp stamp on her back and a black girl's butt named Shayla. I have seen her before in a carnal matter... and she seems just what I need. Since she's on the stage, I quickly leave holding up ten fingers to let her know I will be back in ten minutes.... as I walk out my manhood is starting to rise and I can't wait to get back.... I quickly visit 7 other bars and nothing compares to Shayla so I cross back from Groove and head back into Passion that looks neon even in the middle of the day. As I walk in, Jimmy the bartender immediately begins pouring my favorite Jack and Coke as soon as our eyes meet. I take my seat in a corner as a young light skinned black girl takes a twirl on the pole in the center of the stage. I don't see Shayla. I assume she's wiping sweat off her after her pole routine. I concentrate on the black girl on stage. She seems to be tricking that body just for me. As she drops to all fours and points that booty at me as she slowly rocks back and forth and pulls her green thong aside to show me her bearded clam or in this case shaven clam I drop three or four ones on her. I can almost smell the sweet pussy she has from the stool... Lord I just wish my tongue was long enough. I would roll it out from here till it reached that sweet cunny she got. Just then I'm jolted out of my reverie by a touch on my arm and it's Shayla. She has put on a halter-top and micro short shorts and sits down by me... Hi JD... how you doing? Can you by me a drink?"

I say "sure" just as her drink is set down. She takes her left hand and reaches for it and takes her right hand and reaches for my cock which I have unleashed from my pants. As we talk about the Orioles and the Ravens, she slowly rubs my cock. Shayla has this down to a science. When I'm just close to my nut, she stops and lo and behold her drink is empty (to the uninitiated in Baltimore strip clubs, your time with a girl expires when she finishes the drink you buy her.) I weakly nod to the bartender for another. Three minutes in and I blow like a smoke stack. Shayla smiles, writes her number down on a napkin. "Call me, JD. I miss having fun with you. Didn't you like it when you took me and Jelly out to the mall?" (Jelly is her four-year-old biracial daughter.) In other words, buy my daughter some clothes and I will suck you and fuck you into a coma

I say, "Well, how is Saturday? Y'all still live in the same place." I say, "How about you just bring her sizes and I bring my wallet and some condoms and we have a ball?" Shayla frowns. The reality is that she likes me and wants me in her life for real instead of just a fuck. As I arrange my clothes, I say "You know what. Forget that. Bring Jelly we'll make a day of it and I will take my two best girls out to the movies after we finish shopping." She smiles as bright as Christmas tree lights. She grabs my neck and pulls me towards her and plants a long slow kiss on me (now to the uninitiated that would have turned my stomach a few years ago because you don't know if these girls just finished sucking somebody's dick but I know that probably isn't the case with Shayla. She charges high to everyone but me so unless they want to pay her what they could pay ten girls for a threesome the only thing they can get from her is a hand job.) Just at that moment, my neck starts to itch where she grabbed it. We say our goodbyes and I head out. As I walk out I notice a drop of white cum like substance on my pants. Who gives a shit? I walk briskly up MLK Street headed back to the courthouse. As I walk, I pull out a spray can of Brut by Faberge and give myself an air bath in the deodorant. As I do that, a few middle-aged women walk by and wrinkle their noses at me about the smell of the deodorant. I wrinkle my face back at them and say to myself "nosy bitches, I don't care what you think. I damn sure don't want to fuck you. Peace out." I walk quickly pass the metal detectors and flash my green attorney's bar pass at the deputies manning the entrance. I walk up the stairs to the second floor and walk by the courtroom as I have 3 and half minutes before the judge takes the bench. I walk to the sink to splash cool water on my face. I look up and I'm startled at what I see. My jowls are hanging loose, my skin looks waxy, and my teeth look ever so more pointier. I have a sheen of dark hair over my head that is usually skin clean. I do not resemble a vampire. I'm resembling nothing more than a gutter rat in a suit and wearing glasses. I remember not just a few years ago that when I looked in the mirror I saw a strong family man. Not the subhuman that I was presented with in the mirror today. I felt almost like crying. I hunched over and gave a strangled sob. Staring at my face, it's like I'm looking in a window at another person not looking in a mirror at myself. I trudge into the courtroom with droplets of water on my shirt and suit and the still ever present white stain from my time with Shayla. I slump down in my chair as the rest of the trial party arrives and of course Billy in chains... I think he should change his name from Billy Badass to Billy Rotten Ass if he lets his rear end lie detector go off one more time I'm gonna faint.... what the hell are the feeding him in jail...

Billy reaches over once he sits down and is freed from his shackles... "Yo JD, you got this. I'm paying you a lot of money. You gotta do this thing for me, for real, yo."

I look at him with a bored face and say... "Have you ever seen me not handle business?... Sit your ass back down and let me handle this."

At that, Billy leans back smiles and says, "My nigga... go get them."

The judge comes in and gavels the case back into order and everyone takes their place ... I walk up to the podium and stare at Elvira. She starts to fidget in her seat swaying from side to side and then she pulls her short skirt down. I can see this through the gap in which she walked in to the witness stand and her fuchsia panty covered crotch is staring at me... I begin. "Elvira, you don't mind if I call you Elvira, do you?"

"Not if you don't mind me calling you JD."....

I smile and say, "You know my name right?"

"Yes."

"You know a lot of lawyers, right?"

"Yes, but not as well as I'd like too." There are titters of laughter and she licks her tongue lasciviously across her lips.

"In fact, you know the attorneys in the prosecutor's office better than all the other attorneys combined?"

"What do you mean by that?"

"Well, you work with them all the time right?"

"Who me? No, I'm not no snitch. I'm real with mine.".

"Well you testified in 5 trials last year correct?"

"Yeah."

"And you testified in 4 trials the year before, right? And in fact you testified in a total of 30 trials in the last 8 years?"

"I guess that's right."

"You in fact were called as a prosecution witness in every last one of those cases right. And each time you just happened to see everything that happened in those cases right?"

"Well yeah, but I was just lucky I guess."

"You were lucky to witness crime? Do most people consider themselves lucky to witness crime? Wouldn't that be unlucky Elvira?"

"Well yes, I mean you know, I don't know what I mean..."

"Elvira," I say as I walk over to my trial table and grab a sheaf of papers. "You declared $20,000 in income last year correct?"

"Yeah that sounds right I don't do my own taxes. The Jew guy on Mosher does my taxes."

"Well do you dispute that amount?"

"No, but I can't say one hundred percent."

"Well you can dispute that 100 percent of every dollar you made that year came directly from crime stoppers correct."

"Well, I'm not sure."

I take her last year's tax return and I stick a green 1 sticker on it and hand it to the court reporter. "Your honor may I show the witness def 1 for identification..."

"Go ahead," says Judge P....

"This is def 1 for id. Do you recognize it, Elvira?

"Not really. It seems to be a tax return." She is sweating so bad, her mascara and powder makeup on her face is starting to run....

"Is it your tax return?

"I don't know."

"Well, look at line three. Is that your social security number?"

"Yes. "

"Is that your name?"

"Yes. Is that your address?"

"It was last year."

"Well, is that your signature at the bottom?"

"Naw it doesn't seem to be. My handwriting is neater than that."

I walk back over to the trial table. I take a second document and mark it as def 2 for id. And once again the judge allows me to approach. I show the exhibit to Elvira. "Do you recognize def 2 for id?"

"Hell yeah," she says in her cigarette ravaged voice. "Everything I just said is in here."

I smiled and asked her, "Do you recognize the signature on the last page?"

She says, "Hell" then her voice drops off as she realizes that the signature on the statement is the exact same as the signature on the 1040 tax form... her face turns red ... she sputters and spittle flies out of her mouth. "You tricked me JD, you son of a bitch," and she starts screaming, "Now the DA's are never gonna pay me no more. You took my livelihood." She is screaming at the top of her lungs.

The judge bangs his gavel and yells "Order.". The deputies grab Elvira and drag her out of the courtroom head first with her red hooker heels dragging she is cursing all the way. Order is restored. Yao is holding his head in his hands and the judge is sitting there seething. As peace and order is restored, I ask permission to publish the signatures to the jury since the witness is no longer available answer questions. Yao objects but shrinks before Judge P.'s glare and slinks back behind his desk and withdraws his objection. The jury looks at the two signatures and many shake their heads in downright disgust at the witness who just tried to bullshit them...

Man, I'm in my hay day. I have dinner with my Carmen and I just tore up a witness like I used to. Feels good son. It shonuff feels good. Yao asks that we be allowed to adjourn until tomorrow when he will call his last witness, Jeremiah Johnson. There is that name again. I feel the hairs on the back of my neck stand up. I can't place that name but ok let me enjoy tonight. Fuck Jeremiah was a bullfrog. I got my shit.... We all stand as the bailiff ends court for the day. Judge P.. angrily slings his gavel on his desk and stalks out and says, "Gentlemen, I will see you tomorrow morning (and no excuses or bring your wallets out.)

CHAPTER 10

Carmen's Tragedy

IT'S A QUARTER TO EIGHT and I'm outside the front of my building. I'm cleanly shaved, both face and head. I'm wearing Cool Water cologne and my only fresh pressed suit, which is a tan ensemble with a royal blue shirt. I have on my Stacy Adams boots and I'm looking like a million bucks (oh, I forgot since the divorce half of everything is my ex's so I guess my look is only worth $500,000 to me.) I see a new Toyota Corolla pull up to the steps and down rolls the passenger window and there sits Carmen with a blinding smile. She says "Hey sailor, do you know where a lady can get a good time for twenty bucks with a giggle on the end?"

I reply, "Be careful on this street. Somebody might think you're serious."

For just an instant a look of panic sets in her eyes. Then she sees my face trying to restrain the laughter within me and she says "Hey no fair; no teasing me before you give me a hug." I hop up off the stairs and I'm in the Corolla in a flash. Carmen gives me a warm hug the kind of hug that is a promise of something more. (To the uninitiated there are hugs when a woman holds her body away from you that are meant as friendly but not at all sexual; there are hello get to know you hugs where her body might press against you for a second... then there are the kind of hugs that Carmen gave me... I don't know how she did it but it seems as if she climbed over in to the passenger seat and pressed her full body against me as if she was in my lap and then she held for a three count until a car behind us honked... when she let go I was flustered.) It's hard for a reprobate like me to be flustered but I was. It had been a long time since something as innocent as a hug had given me not just a sexual but an emotional arousal as well. I better be careful this girl is working with some serious mojo. A woman like this could turn an old player like me into a husband again. As she drives to the harbor, I just concentrate on the sensation of holding her hand. It feels so intense it's almost like my hand is being burned by an ice-cold fire. It's electric cool and hot all at the same time. Every time I turn to look at her in amazement, she just gives me a smile that shows her pearly whites and the two cutest dimples you have ever seen. I'm finally catching my breath and I'm able to gain a little composure so I can spit my game at this girl... but every time I'm ready to do that she gives my hand a little squeeze and I'm right back where I started. Carmen parks the car, turns her head to me, gives me another smile, and says come on the game is starting in a few minutes... She hops out of the car. I realize for the first time she is wearing tight apple bottom black jeans and a ripped to be sewn tighter to her body purple Ray Lewis Ravens jersey... I look around... man she had me so knocked out I didn't even realize that we had not driven to the harbor.

We at Ray Lewis's Steakhouse. Mannnnnnnn......that's good. Is this woman a sorceress? That's when I see her soft brown calfskin boots with 2 1/4 inch heels. Those boots have her assets position in such an angle that I literally get weak in the knees. As we enter the restaurant, Carmen turns on her million watt smile on the maître d' who immediately escorts us to a good table not the best in the house but damn better than I ever got here. I grab a seat forgetting to her help get seated. She gives a little frown and pulls her chair up to the table... I ask her," Did you give that guy a couple hundred bucks? Every time I come here, I have to sit at least an hour and a half for a table and it's almost always by the swing door of the kitchen or next to the bathroom". She giggles and says," No money. I just helped him in a divorce case. He got to keep his boat which his ex wanted to take and burn at sea. You do a good job for people and they will take care of you. So, JD, is this better than Hooters?" I say, " Hell yeah!!" "I hope you know I'm not a Hooters type of girl... if we are going to be seeing each other remember no McDonald's think FRIDAYS ... no Hooters think steak house...no movies think the theater...and when you think of intimacy don't think quick fuck think of a symphony of intimacy... I'm not a simple girl but I'm worth it.", she says. She lays her chin on her hands, which are clasped together braced on the table, and grins like the Cheshire cat. Man how can I ever spit game at this woman when she keeps throwing me off my game? Carmen says one last thing, "Don't slick talk me talk to me like I'm human if you want to get to know me. Game turns me off and you're not the type of man with game you're the type of man who is sincere. You're a husband type not a player, so don't try to be with me, K?"

The air goes out of my sails so much that there is an audible whoosh as the oxygen leaves my lungs...I gather myself and said ok. "Carmen I'll be real... so tell me about you??" She looks away quickly almost dismissively. She looks off to the left away from our table and says, "You really don't want to know ... if you do, let me know ... it's not a blueprint to my panties if that's what you're looking for, but maybe a blueprint to understanding me. Is that what you want Jasper???" I reply, "Yes, it is but call me JD."... She then says forcefully, "No, I won't call you JD. Your mother didn't name you that. She named you Jasper and you should be proud of that and honor her by making people address you by the name she gave you not some acronym that stands for drunken debauchery." My ears burn and sting all at the same time as she says that.... I gulp hard and say," You're right, I guess. I have never thought about it like that. Ok, call me Jasper. Yes, Carmen, I would like to really to get to know you". Just then the waiter comes to the table with water and menus for us.

As he rattles off the specials, I can hear nothing. I'm just enraptured watching Carmen give all the right cultural responses the way she smiles; laughs at the waiter's bad jokes; how she pays rapt attention to his recitation of the specials; and how she asks thoughtful questions of him about the menu. I just have never had the social skills or patience to do any of those things. I'm not the person she is and I see that ... I aspire to be like her, but I wonder if she simply is too good for me. As I sit there and the name Jeremiah Johnson keeps creeping into my mind. It bothers me. I should be working on the trial, but fuck that I'm here with Carmen and she needs and deserves my attention so I push that name on my mind and I just watch her in amazement I just can't see what such an amazing woman could see in me. I'm a nobody, a peon, a loser whose single redeeming quality is my career as a criminal defense attorney. As the waiter leaves, Carmen says "Pick your meal and I'll tell you my story"... I quickly slam my menu shut as the waiter returns to the table, not more than 30 seconds later. I'm sure like everyone else he just wants to be in Carmen's presence. I tell the waiter to bring me a ribeye steak butterflied and well done and loaded baked potatoes and broccoli...

Carmen orders the salmon and as the waiter takes our menus, I see a smirk on Carmen's face. I ask what "What's wrong baby? She says, "That's the exact same thing you ordered at the jazz club the night we met? Don't you ever go for something different. Don't you change sometimes?" I guess the double meaning of what she says goes over my head because I think stupidly that the question is only in regards to food so I answer, "Nope I'm a creature of habit. Don't you know you can't teach an old dog new tricks. I am the man who I am. "She looks a little sad.

As the waiter returns with our drinks, red wine for Carmen and a double Jack and Coke for me... she says, "Well where do I began? I don't think you want to know where I come from. You already know that". I said "True, I want to know what makes you Carmen. What is your essence?" Carmen looks down at the table for some reason. She has the straw from my Jack and Coke and she is playing with it. The ice cubes in my drink clink as she takes a heavy sigh." You don't know, but when I lived in New York I was married. I had three kids and a husband I had my own little solo practice, doing pretty much what I do now. I thought I had the ultimate happy home. My husband and I weren't intimate as much as we used to be, but we still had a family to raise. I loved him and he loved me. I thought.... thought all crumbled to the ground when I got up one morning and read in the headlines of the NY post that my husband was in trouble for having sex in his car with the wife of his company CEO... it wasn't just sex it was alleged as rape...rape. The story said that there had been an ongoing sexual relationship between them for three years and that there had been an abortion during the affair." As tears stream down Carmen's face, I attempt to wipe her tears away, but she violently pushes my arm away and says," No, please just let me finish this story", in a little girl voice that I have never heard from her before. I'm sitting there looking at the paper at the dining room table. I hear my kids in their room upstairs playing and laughing...

I'm sad stunned and astonished at all the same time for three years he has been with another woman living ,laughing ,making love and I didn't know ... I knew he hadn't been home last night. He said he was in Florida working on a deal but according to the Post he was in Westchester County with a woman who wasn't me and now he was in the Westchester jail awaiting arraignment on rape charges. I grabbed my kids and stuck them in the minivan. My mom came with me and when we got to the jail I was in my night gown and robe my eyes were red from crying and my kids where scared and near tears not knowing what was going on and why mommy was so hysterical... as I waited with them in the jail visitation room. James came toward the room in and orange jumpsuit with the words Westchester County Jail stenciled on it. When he saw it was me and the kids, he refused the visit and slunk back to his cell".... "He couldn't face you huh?", I replied inquisitively.   Carmen wrings her hands and tries to smile, but the tears are still flowing and she is still so sad.... I went home and I stayed in bed for the next month; my practice feel apart... my mom had to move in and take care of my kids... as it came out later the rape charges where a false allegation.   The woman said that because she had gotten caught by her husband and she let the police throw James in jail in an attempt to save her family. He was released after 90 days in jail. He sued the boss and her wife and they settled out of court for a few million ...he tried to come back and be in my life but I could not deal with the shame he brought on himself and his family. I can't believe the betrayal he perpetrated on his family and me. Now, I can't even stand to see his face. At first I blamed myself, maybe I wasn't enough woman for him maybe I wasn't sexual enough maybe I wasn't attentive enough ,but through therapy I came to know no one woman was sexual enough for him and that I couldn't be with him anymore. So I packed up and moved here to Baltimore. He still tries to visit the kids and to send me money which I refuse. I divorced him and sold the house in New York. I live comfortably in Baltimore over near Loyola... big house, but its empty because even though I have my kids, I go to bed alone and wake up alone and I just would like someone to love and be loved by. She wrinkles her shoulders by twisting her body to the right and says, "Do you think I'm damaged goods now? Or you think I'm not enough woman for you or anybody else?"

As tears stream down her face... I get up from my chair. I cup her face in my hands, wipe away her tears, and kiss her forehead and tell you more own than I ever dreamed I deserves. And I pray that I can be the man that protects you and makes you happy. She smiles pulls her chair closer to me and says, " I need you by my side." We spent the rest of dinner with her head leaning on my shoulder talking small talk playing with our food and ruminating over life. Shortly after 10:30, we leave and she zooms down the highway bringing us back to Baltimore proper and to my apartment. As she pulls up we sit in the car. I ask if she wants to come in. She laughs and said "I told you I'm not that type of girl. If you want me and all this" ,which she uses her right hand to display her body "You gotta do more than hear my sad story and eat a steak with me."

She pecks me on my cheek and says, "Now get out!" with a grin on her face. As I stand outside, I walk over to her driver's side and I give her a longer kiss on her lips and say to her ... "What do I have to do to have all that?"

"You got to figure that out, Jasper. If you can't get to know me enough to know how to signal to me that you're ready to be the man in my life; the husband that I deserve ; then I'm not gonna tell you how to do that. You have got to earn that knowledge not be given it." As I stand up she pulls off and I watch her ...I stand in the road watching her until I hear the horn from the Baltimore light rail and I see the train coming up behind me quick. I move off to the side walk quickly.... I walk into my building and as I get to my door, I see a note on the door from Yun who was the shorter of the two Asian girls I had just had my adventure(when, the night before???)... The note said: "After you get off your date with that cute black girl, why don't you invite her to join us or you can just come over tonight and I can suck your dick. I'll be up late doing homework just come knock." I crumple the note up with indignation at the thought of touching Carmen with perversion, makes me extremely angry... at least at first. I undress and go to bed. That thought makes me hotter and hotter. I get so hot that no masturbation is going to handle what I'm going thru. I throw on my robe and tie the cord on my pajama bottoms...I grab my key s and before I know it I'm at Yun's door.... she opens that door not looking like a vixen but a tired college student with no makeup her hair pulled back in a ponytail and thick black glasses. I'm almost taken aback... she looks weary, but she laughs, leads me into her private room, and sits me in a lazy boy chair before the fireplace. She strips down to her lacy red Victoria's Secret undies (What's left is covered by that little amount of thread ain't much of a secret.) and she proceeds to give me the best blow job of my life... as I sit there the cell phone in my pocket rings and I look at the number as Yun uses her teeth in disapproval. I say shush just pretend I'm Bill Clinton and I look at the number it's Carmen. I shut my eyes and answer the phone. Carmen asks, "What do you have on?"

I tell her I have on pajama bottoms and that's it. She says I have on my little rainbow striped panties and they are soaked thinking about you... She gives a low moan in to the phone. I shut my eyes and pretend that Yun's mouth belongs to Carmen. I start groaning Carmen oh fuck Carmen... she starts moaning as well and within 75 seconds I'm screaming and cumming and yelling Carmen Carmen Carmen. And Carmen meows like a kitty cat and there is a hitch in her breath as she releases too. She asks me was that good for you I say hell yeah (she just has no idea and says goodnight Jasper I'm really falling for you and I say goodnight. I click the phone shut and look down at Yun. She smiles,

"Don't worry I'm not jealous I saw her earlier. You should get her to join us she looks yummy... now get out I gotta get back to my homework I have a test tomorrow and you just gave me the break I needed, but it's time to get back to work... now shoo. I walk or limp rather back to my home... I'm so tired that I sleep a dreamless sleep so tired I couldn't dream I wanted to dream of Carmen and love but I can't, so sleep I do.

CHAPTER 11

Mr. GrayBoy Returns

INEFFECTIVE ASSISTANCE OF COUNSEL... That's all I can think about this morning. Why didn't I keep my ass at home instead of going out with Carmen? Even better, why didn't I go work on the case instead of getting a blowjob from Yun? Man, I'm a dumb ass. I dress hurriedly. I just don't know who the fuck Jeremiah Johnson is and why didn't I have my pi investigate it. Shit, I don't like being unprepared. I can't find a clean suit so I throw on my suit from last night and the shirt I had on as well. I see a little steak sauce stain on the left shirt pocket but fuck it. I'll have on a jacket all day. I get dressed ; grab my bag and head towards the courthouse. Shit, I forgot to grab my Tylenol and I feel a monster headache coming on. I walk to the courthouse for the first time in a while I'm unsure. I usually walk in and I'm ready for court no matter what but I let things slip and I'm not ready. I swear to God that if he will let me make it through this day I'll never go to court again without being ready for trial. Fuck. I have a feeling of dread as I go into court. As everyone comes in, Billy is unshackled and sits next to me. He asked, "Yo JD, who the fuck is Jeremiah Johnson? I don't know that muthafucka and how do he know me?" As the judge and jury file in, Billy keeps asking me the same question. I don't answer him I just keep looking forward and acting like I don't know what the fuck he is saying. I have my Joe cool look on and I'm twirling a pencil in between my fingers. I'm all cool and relaxed. If you can't make it, fake it. So I'm totally unprepared when Yao stands up and asks to approach the bench. As we walk up to the bench, I look back at my former homie, Head, sitting at the prosecution table. He has an evil grin on his face. He then mimics a man throwing down a shot of alcohol most likely Jack down his throat... ok Head I'll fuck you over later I think to myself. When we arrive at the bench, Yao tells Judge P. that he needs to have the courtroom cleared because Mr. Johnson, the next witness he plans to call is an undercover agent for the DEA. He requests that the court seal the courtroom for his testimony. On the belief that if he testified in open court it will damage ongoing investigations and could cost this agent his life. Judge P. looks at me and I state, "Your honor, my client has the right to confront his accusers. He has a right to a public trial. If the prosecution feels that this witness is necessary, then they have to subject him to the same public scrutiny as any witness that I call would be. Being an officer is nothing special and deserves no special protection. At his statement, Judge P. raises his eyebrows.

Aw crap, I forgot he was a cop before he became a lawyer. Sugar honey ice tea, I know what's coming next. "Nothing special, huh counselor? Is that your position, Mr. Davis", spits Judge P.. I say, "Ummm yeah that's it judge". The judge turns to the bailiff "Jody seal the courtroom. Right now." All the family, friends and professional court watchers grumble and move towards the door. Attorneys watching the trial look stunned as they are asked to leave, too. I notice one of them is Carmen and she blows me kisses as she walks out. As I look at her, I notice an eye twitch that I have never seen before. What's up with that? The hair on the back of my neck is standing up and I feel a cold sweat coming down my face. As soon as the court is cleared the judge explains to the jury that the next witness is an undercover agent and the courtroom has been cleared in the interest of keeping that agent safe and to protect ongoing investigations. I say a silent curse to myself. Not only has Judge P. cleared the courtroom, but he has made this witness become Serpico before he ever testifies. They are gonna believe every fucking word that he says. Oh hell, just get ready to go toe to toe... Yao stands up and says that he calls Jeremiah Johnson, special agent of the DEA... In walks a tall, pale shaved head, white man in a goatee. He is wearing dark blue slacks, blue shirt, and tweed jacket with patches on the sleeves. He is sans ties and wearing conservative black frame rims. Why the fuck does he seem so familiar? I can't place it. Well I couldn't until he got on the witness stand and answered I do to the question about to tell the truth the whole truth and nothing but the truth. Dammit, I know that voice but it doesn't fit the appearance that's fucking GrayBoy, Mr. GrayBoy. Shit what the fuck? I've partied with him before with hookers and a mound of white powder. I personally saw him imbibe of that white shit snow in his Reservoir Hill brownstone mansion. I've seen him beat a man down with a baseball bat for mistreating one of his girls. Oh, I'm going to get this mutherfucker but then my heart drops. He's seen me imbibe in coke as well off the belly of his girl Nandi, his bottom bitch (for the uninitiated that means his main girl). In fact, he told me that he would give me his girls anytime I wanted if I would agree to be his private attorney. You know sex for legal fees.

My mind is racing a mile a minute. I know I said no to his offer. It was a huge struggle for me, but pussy is everywhere and I knew that GrayBoy would be up on murder charges soon because of how violent and arrogant he seemed to be. If I bury him on the stand, he can bury my career, my life, and take my law license. He could take all of what little I have left. What the fuck am I gonna do? Why couldn't I keep my prick in my pants? Why couldn't I resist the coke/ I've never used coke before that day and never after but this guy probably has me on video tape. As GrayBoy' settles in the witness chair, he looks at me not with a smile, not with a glare, but a simple inquisitive look. As if to say do you really want to go after me, so I have to lay your whole life bear before this courtroom? I can't think I'm damn near catatonic. My amazement is only matched by my client, Billy. His ass truth detector is working overtime the smell is so bad I believe that he has shit on himself. I'm probably not smelling any better than he is right now. We make such a pair, scared and more scared. This is where my life has been heading. I'm trapped between my duty to my client and my instinct of self-preservation. Scylla and fucking Charybdis, this feels like an out of body experience. My voice squeaks barely above the level of a stage whisper ."Your honor, may we approach?" Judge P. turns a baleful look at me and holds it for a full thirty seconds before he says the word I need. "Approach."

"Your honor, this is a surprise witness. This undercover should have been disclosed months ago. It's not fair your honor. This witness should not be allowed to testify."

Yao replies directly to me. "Fair? JD, no one would ever accuse you of ever being fair. "

Judge P. says, "Shut up. Both of you. Counsel this could have been discovered through motion practice which you always seem to never do in any case I see. I've never seen you file a motion and the appropriate motion would have been a bill of particulars. I'm going to give you a one day continuance to get your shit together, Mr. Davis.   When   we reconvene you better be ready or I will drop the letter I prepared to bar counsel regarding your behavior in the mail overnight express ... and Mr. Yao, return to your table."

"Your honor and ex parte conversation? "

"Yes, sit your ass down.' replies Judge P.. Yao seems to skip to his table he is so elated. "JD, I had high hopes for you but you've failed that. I can smell the liquor coming from your pores. You don't have any more chances with me. Get your shit together, before I get your meal ticket taken away. You've got some soul searching to do and I urge you to get it together right now. Now step back." I walk back to the defense table visibly shaken. I don't know what I can do or where I'm going. Billy looks shaken. I'm shaken. I look over at the prosecution table and Head is laughing and Yao has a serene look on his face as if he pities me. All I can think of is what GrayBoy has told the prosecutors about me. Judge P. announces to the jury that there are some legal issues that have to be addressed and that the jury is excused until 9:30 am tomorrow, with that he bangs his gavel and walks out. Slowly, the jury files out as well. The deputies grab up Billy and walk him out in shackles. Yao and Head walk out. They both look at me and shake their heads. Soon I'm the only person in the courtroom unless you account for the demons that are surrounding me. I'm lost.

CHAPTER 12

A Day with Myself

THE TIME IS NOON I'm sitting in my office for the first time in two weeks. Christy comes in to see if I want a blowjob and I wave her away. I open the drawer to my desk and pull out a bottle of 99 Bananas 99 proof alcohol. I don't drink it. I just look at the bottle. I feel like a child. I want to cry, but I can't summon the tears. I'm paralyzed by my own actions.

Jeff comes in, " JD, What's good bro, how is the trial going??" In fact, what are you doing in the office today?" I tell Jeff to grab a seat and sit down. As he shuts the door, I let it all pour out about my interactions with GrayBoy and my sinking feeling of being revealed. I'm damn near in tears. Jeff leans back in his chair with his hands clasped behind his head. He gives a little humm. I can't be sure what his face reveals, because my face was lying in my hands on my desk. I feel tears leak through my fingers. Will my son read about his perverted scumbag father in the paper or see me on Fox news? Will I ever be able to support him and my ex the way they deserve? I had shamed my whole family. My whole life is a shambles. I'm lost.

Jeff says, "Hey, JD what you did is bad but it seems worse became it is a secret. Your life has been a secret; therefore, the possibility of the revelation of it is scarier than the actuality. All he can really say is you sniffed coke and that was with him. He can't admit that or he looks like a drug fiend. He can say you slept with hookers, but so did he. He can say you agreed to represent him for sex with his hookers, but where is the proof. As far as I know we have never had a case with him and you and I have been partners for years (I hid the cases and fees from

Jeff).... What's scaring you is what you could have done not what you actually did. "I sit back in my chair and take in what Jeff has just said ...

"Jeff you have always been my best friend and you have always been able to put my life in perspective."

"JD when this is over get yourself some help or I can't be your partner anymore. It's bad enough that my wife won't let me hang out with you anymore because she knows your proclivities. Now, you are losing who you are as a man. Remember back in high school, when we both agreed that when we reached this age we both just wanted to be husbands and fathers. We were gonna leave the pussy chasing to the idiots who want to be alone in their old age? Jasper, you're damn close to being that lonely old man. Get yourself together." Somehow all of that goes in one ear and out the other. I say thanks bro and rushed Jeff out. I call Christy in and I'm rejuvenated. As Christy drops to her knees, I start plotting my rebirth and my cross of GrayBoy a.k.a. Jeremiah Johnson. Wait until he gets a load of me! I'm going to tear him a new asshole. I give a grunt as Christy finishes me off. She smiles as I give her forty bucks out of my wallet. As she leaves, I decide I need to go home and get a good rest and plot my revenge. I mean cross exam of GrayBoy. Shit, maybe I can go down to the block and confirm my weekend date with Shayla. Since today is Friday. What looked like a bad day is gonna be ok after all. I slam my laptop shut and yell to Christy that I'm gonna work from home for the rest of day. "I got a witness to slaughter tomorrow and I gotta focus." She smiles and as I walk out, I yell to Jeff, "Thanks bro, I owe you one man! "

Jeff replies, "No you owe me a million and one day I'm going to collect. So take care of your mangy hide so there is something left to collect." I walk down Baltimore Street towards the Block, as I stroll I'm thinking of mood music to destroy GrayBoy by. The recurrent theme in my head is "Who We Be" by DMX. But for some reason, every time I let my mind wander I keep hearing Bone Thugs in Harmony singing "Meet You At The Crossroads". Curious. Is my subconscious trying to tell me something? Am I at a crossroads in my life? Is this my last chance to make the right turn and have a good and fruitful life? As I walk, I get winded not physically but my spirit is sagging. How many women? How much liquor? How much partying can I live through and come through on the other side? As I contemplate this, I look up and realize I'm at Shayla's bar. I'm tempted to leave and walk away... but I can't I owe Shayla right? She's counting on me to do stuff for her and her child right? If I don't do it; no one else will. I need her and she needs me. She needs her daddy to provide for her. Look, I know that's fucked up logic but my mind is full of the desire to need to be loved and needed. I've always felt alone. So when I think someone needs me (more properly needs my wallet) I get a feeling as if I'm loved. Intellectually, I know Shayla would move on to the next sucker, but I didn't care. It feels good to be needed. It feels good that she needs me so bad that she will do whatever I ask (not beyond reason) her to do. Unless she has something else to do like clean her house wash her hair etc. But hey, it feels good to be needed, ok?

I stop dead on in my tracks instead of going into the bar...I stop and look at my image in the reflective building glass right beside me. I pick up my phone and as I stare at myself I dial Shayla's number. As her voice mail picks up, I hear myself say Shayla I can't do this anymore I need to be by myself and take care of myself. My life has been falling apart and I need to get everything that drains me out of my life. I need to be by myself. I hang up the phone and as I look at myself in the glass I start to smile and for the first time in a long time I see a glimmer of who I used to be reflected back at me. At that moment, I realize what I have to do if I want to regain myself. I have to cut ties to my old life and obsessions... My wife didn't kick me out because she fell out of love with me. She kicked me out because I was no longer the person who married her and loved her and raised a child with her. He was not present in my body anymore. He was replaced by a voracious appetite.

CHRIS SHELLA

I felt tears roll down the corners of my eyes. I was sniffling and crying at the same time... people who walked by me and stared like I was one of the circus freaks (read heroin addicts) that walk the streets of Baltimore. I don't know what the fuck has come over me. Memories of my depravity of the past five years flood back to me. How many you're the daddy baby schemes had I gone through? How many clandestine blackmail schemes had I endured from women who wanted only my money and nothing else. How much had I suffered? Lying awake beside someone who I just wanted to leave my home, but I couldn't because I didn't want to upset them. What the fuck have I done to myself? I walk at a fast pace to my condo...

Whimpering and sniffling the whole way. As I turn my door handle open, my Asian fantasy girls walk by. As they say hi, I display a look of horror on my face and slam the door shut in their faces. This is going to be so hard. How can I let those girls go? They give me so much pleasure. I deserve that pleasure.... as my mind trials off. I snap back to the issue so hard that my neck hurts. I don't deserve them. I deserve peace of mind. I'm getting old and I'm alone I can't continue my life like this. Sex is not a reward for hard work. I lock my door and throw the deadbolt and I walk to my TV. I tuned it to the WORD channel (to the uninitiated, it's a gospel channel) on there I see my Morehouse brother Jamar Bryant giving the word to the people. Man, I let the music and preaching wash over me. I sit in my lazy boy chair scene of so many sexual encounters, that there is a stain of sexual energy emanating from it.

I jump up like it was old Smokey, the famous electric chair for executions.... I sit at my dining room table and I go through my mental Rolodex of phone numbers. I pull out my phone and set it on the table and stare at it. I have a choice I can sit here and prep for Mr. GrayBoy. Or I can sit here and call all these women I'm involved with and cut off the relationships and get the person who I used to be back in my life. I stare at my trial computer and my phone. I had to sit there for an hour looking at the two tools, one for GrayBoy destruction and one for my redemption. As I sit there, a little voice in my head says hey you got a good start by dumping Shayla. Do this slowly and you will get a chance to say goodbye to all the girls and still have goodbye sex.

As that thought percolates in my mind, I slide the phone away and grab the laptop. Just as I write and type away on questions to trip up GrayBoy, I realize I have to take a wicked, wicked Wilson Pickett shit. So I pop up, walk to the bathroom, and plop down on the seat. After I finish my business, I go to the sink, turn on the hot water, and grab a bar of soap to wash my hands. As I wash my hands, I look up at the mirror. I expected to see a glimmer of my former self. I don't see that. I see a demon looking back at me. The expression I see on the mirror is a smile, a grin even , but that is not the expression I feel inside myself. I'm in full horror. I have lost all of myself. I drop the soap. Run back to the table. I slam the computer shut and for the next for hours I'm making calls to the women I have been seeing... Carmen cries and tells me she understands. Angelica curses at me and says she'll get even... Christy, my receptionist, says, "It's ok JD. I'm there when you need me". The Asian girls cry and say we understand Jasper; find yourself...but the door is always open to you. I laugh it off nervously. I make about 20 other calls... at that point I then call ATT and have them change my cell number for me. So now these women can't reach me even if they tried. I rock back in the chair and exhale a sigh of relief... just then I hear a knock on the door. I go to it and there is Trina the stripper from Norma Jeans. She is wearing a trench coat and red stiletto heels.

"Hi, Jasper. How ya doing?"

I blurt out, "If Mohamed won't go to the mountain, then the mountain must go to Mohammed." A blank look covers her face and she says, "Huh?" She steps into my condo without an invitation (not that I tried to hold her out by force She drops her trench coat and she has on only a red bra, panties, and garters that match her stilettos perfectly... I am ready for round two.

"Jasper, why haven't you called me?" Out of the pocket of the coat she pulls out a short whip that she playfully applies to my backside. I'm frozen and don't know what to do... she pushed me into my lazy boy and drops to her knees in front of me. She pulls her long black hair into a ponytail and starts to give me my favorite pleasure. I start to fall back into the chair and then I have a rush of memories and I look down at her and I'll be damned if I don't see the same image I saw in Devil's Advocate with Keanu Reaves. Do you remember the scene where the three demon women are jogging and they are chasing the film's managing partner to kill him and their faces resemble rotting skulls with too many teeth? Immediately, I push her off of me and throw her her coat.

She yells, "Hey, what gives?! What the fuck is you doing? This is bullshit. You know you want this!"

All I can see is the demon head I saw a few seconds ago... I tell her, "This isn't my life anymore. My wife and I reconciled and I'm going to be moving. I can't do this..."

She says, "Well I have some bills to pay. Can you help me, Jasper?"

I empty my wallet and hand it to her. It looks like five hundred cash and I hand it to her. She smiles, puts on her coat and ties the belt of it at her waist and smiling says, "If you ever change your mind, let me know? I could always use the bread."

As she walks out, I close the door, throw the deadbolt, and slide down the door to my butt with my head resting against the cool metal... I glance at my watch and I saw that it was 2 am... man can't prep for GrayBoy now. Fuck it. I'll wing it like I always do. I got skills, hopefully they're still there. I walk to the shower and as it heats up I wash the day's grime and grit and Trina's lipstick off of my Johnson. After 20 minutes of body soaking heat, I get out of the shower. I stand in front of the fogged up mirror and I'm almost afraid to look. I slowly take my right hand and wipe the mirror clean. I first see my eyes, not a stranger's eyes and not a demon's eyes but my own staring back at me.

I see my face a little fatter than it used to be. My nose... My lips... I don't just see a glimmer of myself. I actually see myself.... My expression is sad but I say to myself, "JD, where have you been? It's good to see you again old friend. I have missed you. "I bite my lip, dry off, oil myself down, and throw on a pair of boxer brief underwear and an old t-shirt and I hop in bed. I fall asleep comfortable in my bed and comfortable with myself for the first time in a long time... I sleep the sleep of the restored and for the first time in a long time I'm alone in my bed and alone in my skin and it feels good.

CHAPTER 13

It's been a long time coming

I WAKE UP AND immediately stretch and yawn. That stretching action causes my bed sheets to fall off. I get up and I walk to the bathroom eager to see if my face has changed, eager to see if I'm still myself... I look in the mirror and there I am. A little fuzzy around the edges, but it's definitely Jasper Davis. Badly in need of a shave of both my head and face, I lather up and using my vibrating Fusion razor. I right myself to the image I always have of myself. I do cut myself while trimming up my beard but it feels good. It's honest pain. It's my pain not someone else's. I'm myself not a facsimile and I'm ready to go to war. GrayBoy is in for it. I get dressed. I assess my wardrobe and it looks pretty shabby. I look in the back of the closet. I see zippered up, my closing day suit.. It's a sharp black Zegna suit somber and elegant. I think about it. But you know what? "Never let them see you coming" I know I quote a lot from Devil's Advocate (best trial movie I ever saw). I put on a shabby brown suit that has buttons hanging on by a thread. I pull on my trial boots, grab my trial notebook and laptop, and I'm out the door. It is a bright and warm day. The sun kisses my skin as I walk to the courthouse. I stop down Baltimore Street and I grab a McDonald's breakfast. Eggs, sausage and extra hashbrowns all washed down by a large coke. Man, that felt good. I walk to the courthouse with a spring up the steps that I hadn't had since I was a brand new lawyer eager to get to court and do justice (until I found out justice and what happens in a courthouse are frequently mutually exclusive). I walk into the courtroom I'm fifteen minutes early but the judge is on the bench looking evil and his bench is surrounded by Yao, Head and two federal marshals that I recognize. My client is chained to the trial table looking scared. Judge P.'s voice booms out, "Mr. Davis could you please join us? I quickly walk toward the bench only stopping to leave my briefcase at the trial table but I expected to get an especially raw message from my client's butt lie detector but he is surprisingly fresh and clean." Could you please join us ? "Judge P. booms.

"Coming, your honor." Everyone at the bench is eyeing me suspiciously.

"Good morning your honor. I thought I was early."

"You are Mr. Davis... but we have got some bad news. Agent Jeremiah Johnson was murdered last night in the house he uses in his undercover capacity. Five shots to the head and three to the heart from a 9mm automatic that was left at the scene.

"That's horrible," I exclaim....

"I'm not finished yet Mr. Davis," as the judge leans over the bench towards me... there was a "Stop Snitching dvd shoved into his mouth.(For the uninitiated, "Stop Snitching is a credo, I dare say a movement in Baltimore where people are encouraged strenuously sometimes with guns knives and threats of violence to their families to not to testify against defendants.) "Wow that's crazy...", I say.

Judge P. says "I'm not finished.'

Judge P. roars, "Where were you early this morning between 3 am and 5:30 am?... Tell me which of your sluts you were with so we can get on with the damn trial." The judge's frankness takes me aback.. "

"Judge, I was home alone last night."

"Alone??? JD come on, this isn't the fucking time to be shy these marshals want to take you down to the federal courthouse and question you and probably arraign your ass on federal murder charges involving a witness which carries the death penalty. So just tell us so we can move on...

"I'm telling the truth your honor."

"JD you're not the man I once knew." Judge P. says, "Gentleman, step back."

As we approach our respective trial tables, I feel Yao's and Head's eyes burning a hole in my back. I look at them and they don't turn away. They openly stare. Their eyes asking the question "Were you involved?" I return their gaze with a look of righteous indignation. At that moment, Judge P. tells the bailiff to bring the jury in. inside of four minutes, they are seated and Judge P. tells them we have had difficult legal issues arise and in my discretion I'm going to give you the day off. Giving you a three day weekend since its Friday. The jurors all smile and as they get up, they are in a jovial mood but the second they leave, the dark cloud returns over the court as the judge awaits the jury's departure. After they leave, Yao immediately stands up and says, "I move for a mistrial, your Honor. The state cannot go forward without this crucial witness."

"Mistrial," I say as I stand up. That's fine if they want it but double jeopardy has attached to my client so therefore if they move for a mistrial, they cannot retry these trials at a later date.

Yao yelps, "Your honor... how can the defendant benefit from a mistrial he has caused?"

"Caused?" I say.

Looking incredulously, Judge P. booms, "Sit down both of you." First he looks at Yao. "What proof do you have that Mr. Johnson had anything to do with Mr. Jeremiah Johnson's death??? Huh, what proof?"..

Yao shrinks to about the size of a third grader and says "Nothing yet, your honor, but we will."

Judge P.. growls "Well, don't make charges in my court unless you're willing to back them up. I'm going to close court for the weekend so you can figure out over the weekend what you want to do. I will tell you this though, without some proof of the defendant's or his counsel's complicity in this murder,(I looked shocked) any mistrial motion that is granted will attach double jeopardy to Mr. William Johnson and he cannot be retried. So either rethink your strategy or bring me some proof that he is involved. I look at the judge with a righteous anger that is burning in me and he looks back with a face of disappointment. We stare each other down until he turns his head away and states "This case is continued until Monday morning." The court clerk gets up and states "God save this state and this honorable court," and with that Judge P. blows out of the courtroom. I look at Billy and he gives me an evil grin. He hasn't done his usual questioning act. He hasn't asked me a damn thing but for the first time all trial he looks mutherfucking happy. This bitch ass nigga is smiling. Right then, I know he had something to do with GrayBoy meeting his untimely end. Head walks over to my table and says, "JD, I know you have been through a lot and I know you have been around the criminal scumbag mutherfuckers a lot. But tell me you didn't do this man. Tell me you ain't a mutherfucking criminal."

I look at him and say, "Do you really think I am a criminal? You used to be my boy. Do these suckers have you so turned around that you believe I would be involved with your shit?"

"JD, I've seen your FBI file. I don't know what you would be involved with anymore I just don't know."

Now it's my time to be speechless. As Head walks away, the two US Marshals who were at the judge's bench when I walked in come to my table. "Mr. Davis, would you mind accompanying us back to our office? We have some questions we would like to ask you regarding Mr. Johnson's death."

... I reply "Hell yeah, I would mind talking with you... I am not under arrest am I?"

"No sir, you are not but it's interesting that you would phrase that question that way sir."

I look at him and say "Fuck you G-man, I'm not going anywhere with any of you.".... I look back and I see a huge black man with a tight Caesar fade. He has both of his hands gripping the rail of the bar. He is literally shaking with fury and he is staring directly at me. The feds say that is Mr. Johnson's partner with the DEA and he would like to have a word with you. "So you guys are gonna play good cop, bad cop. Go ahead let him attack me. I will have News Five down here so fast that your head will swim." ... They glare and walk away... I say to their retreating backs, "Go ahead take your attack Negro with you unless you want to see him in jail in the next fifteen minutes." ...I gesture toward the courtroom deputies who are fingering their side arms as they look at the dead man's partner. The marshals take that in as well (I guess supplying the alcohol to the deputies' Christmas parties is paying off). They say to him "Come on Tom, this investigation is going to heat up this weekend and we will get to Jack Daniels later." They say my nickname with such venom you would think it was a curse word. As the courtroom clears, I wait and give them a fifteen-minute head start to clear the area. I start to thank the marshals...but they say, "Don't thank us," says John Selby the senior courtroom deputy. "We were doing our job and if it turns out you did this shit we are gonna whoop your ass when we get you downstairs in the pens... we don't play that kill a cop bullshit. Watch yourself JD or I'm gonna put my foot so far up your ass that you're gonna taste shoe leather... now get out of here. I quickly pack my briefcase after I am able to catch my breath... don't let the smooth taste fool you I'm scared shitless. For the first time in years, I spent the night alone and have no one to alibi me. I walk out of the courtroom like an undead zombie. Is it my imagination or is everyone staring at me? As I turn the corner for the outside door every form of media that you can imagine immediately mobs me. Everyone from the Baltimore Sun to the Washington Post to the City Paper to even a crew from TMZ all asking me questions about the murder of Jeremiah Johnson aka GrayBoy... This throng is so tight that I can barely move. Usually in cases like this the deputies would intervene and push these media assholes off of me but I guess bad news travels fast and they just stood there and smirked at me. Now under Maryland law, an attorney cannot comment on a case beyond asserting the fact that a client has entered a plea of not guilty but I'm being swamped. I'm scared about proving my innocence and I'm alone and I don't even have a woman to provide me comfort because I pushed them all away from me last night.... "My client is innocent and I'm innocent...I resent the statements and assertions of the prosecutor in fact I would ask them where they were last night and who they were with and I challenge them to answer the fucking question!" with those words and a flourish of my trial bag I clear the media hit the steps and head towards my apartment... I'm a jumble of thoughtful recriminations. All I can think of is if you lie down with dogs you come up with fleas and I'm itching like a mutherfucker. Shit why did this have to happen? Why didn't I stay with my Asian fantasy last night? why did I kick Trina out? I can't fucking win. I can't fucking win... On the way home, I stop and pick up a pint of Gentleman Jack and the second I clear the door of the liquor store, I rip the black plastic of the bottle, unscrew the cap, and let the golden liquor roll down my throat. The burn in my throat tells me I'm still alive. I screw the cap back on and cross the street to my condo building. I'm so fidgety that I can't wait for the elevator. I bound up the stairs two at a time. I shove my key in my door and once I'm in, I slam the door, and shoot the deadbolt. I sling my bag to the floor and drop in my lazy boy, lay my head back and cover my face with my hands what the fuck I'm gonna do. I have to have sat there at least five hours. I must have fallen asleep. I awake to a knock at my door... I groggily get up and at the door is an US Marshal serving me with a subpoena to appear before the grand jury Monday morning at nine. "What the fuck is this? I'm in the middle of a first degree murder trial.."..

The marshal replies, ""If you have any questions, call the undersigned AUSA." I took the subpoena and it's not signed by an AUSA but by the US Attorney Mary Jo Butowski. Shit, I'm getting deeper and deeper. I slam the door in his face and I crumple to the floor. Then I think, "What am I panicking for? I haven't done a damn thing wrong. I'm not guilty or involved in the murder anyway so I shouldn't deal with this like this. Why be stressed when I'm innocent?"

I fish my phone out of my pocket with my left hand and dial the number. As I put the phone to my ear, I hear the phone ringing about three times and I announce my name "Hi, this is Jasper Davis."

Before I can finish the receptionist interrupts me and says, "Yeah Mr. Davis, Ms. Butowski was expecting your call. I'll put you right through." As I ring through, sweat beads back up on my brow. Man, this is bull I haven't done anything. The only thing I'm guilty of was being a former sex addict and there is nothing in the US code about that.... Ms. Butowski picks up and says Hi Jasper, how are you (by strange twist of fate Mary and I were fellow line ADA's in Suffolk County New York. I left to defend criminals and she stayed on the dark side of the force. In her defense, she has extremely nice legs for a prosecutor but I digress). "Mary what's going on? You know I had nothing to do with that."

"Jasper, I don't know. ... you're not the same man I learned the law with. Your activities in Baltimore are legion and you associate with the filthiest criminals I know."

"Mary that doesn't make me a killer ... that doesn't make me a conspirator... I'm innocent..."

"Well if you're innocent, why don't you come down to our offices and speak to the investigators looking into the case?"

"Fine," I yell into the phone. "I'll be right there." I grab my trial bag by reflex and I shut off the lights in my condo. As I open the door, I see two thick neck white boys in suits and with earpieces, one with blonde hair and one with red hair. I see the red head one talk directly into the microphone secreted in his jacket.

The blonde guy turns to me and says "Mr. Davis we're your escort to the US attorney's office? We have a car outside to take you there." The feeling of dread is so thick now that I feel it in my throat I can barely breathe. Escorts... how can you escort me when I just decided to go there...Both guys don't respond they just smile a Cheshire cat smile and flex their arms with their hands clasped in front of them."" I say no thank you. It's a few blocks from here I can walk my damn self. As I lock my apartment, I brush by them both, and walk to the stairs. As I round the corner, I can hear their heavy footsteps behind me. As I had brushed by them, I felt the heavy caliber guns they have secure in shoulder holsters under their arms. As I hit the front door and take a right to head to the Fed courthouse, I see that they are maintaining a ten step distance behind me ...still with that damn Cheshire cat smile on them... thoughts start running through my mind what if these guys aren't feds what if the work for the killer. What if they are here to insure that I KEEP MY DAMN MOUTH shut. A ride with them could have ended with me taking a dirt nap... shit.. Get a hold of yourself, JD. As I hit the corner, I take the left and I still see them maintaining the distance... it takes every bit of impulse control I have not to bolt and run for freedom. That's probably what they're hoping for. Flight can be considered an indication of a guilty conscience, under Maryland law. It can be introduced to a jury, if this reaches a trial. Dammit, Jasper stop thinking like a lawyer, think like a human being....after 8 minutes I reach the courthouse front steps and I see my escorts are still at their regulated distance from me. As I look back, they smile and extend their hands gesturing at the courthouse front door. I take a huge sigh of relief and walk through the door. The marshal at the front door asks my name and intentions in the building. I tell him I have an appointment with the US attorney as he makes a call. I take off my sports jacket and metal items and put them through the detector. Right then, I feel the huge patches of sweat that have accumulated at my underarms and back. I'm so soaked; I see sweat stains on my jackets. I know the liquor I drank is sweating out of my pores. I must reek of liquor and all the other toxins that I have imbibed in. My mind screams that smell is who I used to be... I walked away from all the bullshit I'm clean as the driven snow... Jesus has forgiven me that's what pastor Jamar told me, so why can't man forgive me?... My head is ringing at theses inner protestations of innocence. I pass through the metal detector and the marshal directs me to the US Attorney's office. As I collect my wallet from the metal detector screening machine, it falls open and there for the first time in a month I catch a glimpse of the picture of my ex-wife and son. She is so beautiful and I lost her and my son he has been the center of my life but I haven't even bothered to call him for months.. How could I have traded them in for the filth that I have wallowed in the last few years? Man, I traded a Lexus in for a broke down Chevy. What is wrong with me? As I pause I look and see my two escorts cleared security by just showing their credentials, which are encased in twin leather billfolds. They then stand quietly between me and the exit door.

With their hands clasped in front of themselves again. I sigh; take one last glance at my ex-family and I trudge over to the elevators. I pressed the up button and the elevator dings, the door opens and I walk on. My escorts stand at the door and wave bye that damn Cheshire grin still on their face. I guess they figure they did their job and I'm walking to an execution like a condemned man's last walk to the gas chamber. My legs are weak. I sag against the back of the elevator. I bet they're watching me on the camera in the elevator to see what I'm doing that's what they didn't have to ride with me.... how did my life go so bad so fast?

CHAPTER 14

In the Box

THE ELEVATORS DINGS AND I've arrived at the domain of the United States Attorney For The Middle District of Maryland . As I walk in, I wonder, will I be walking out of here the way I walked in, under my own terms or as a guest of the United States in chains and shackles? I take a huge gulp and swing in the doors to the office. There is Head and the two marshals I saw at the courthouse earlier waiting on me. "Good afternoon Mr. Davis. If you will follow us, we can start asking you a few questions", they said. What am I doing as panic sets in again... how many times have I told clients never talk to the police? You are never going to talk you way out of this. Remember that movie with Travolta and Samuel Jackson where Sam Jackson's character says to a college age white boy before he kills him, "My name is Pitt and you ain't talking your way out of this shit." But here I am on the way to talk to federal investigators and one of Baltimore's finest murder police. I don't even have a fucking lawyer with me.. Ok. Ok JD keep it icy if they think they see you nervous and sweating they will believe your lying and try to pin this on you. They escort me into an interrogation room. There are four metal chairs in this precisely square room that is painted dour gray. There is a metal table and one metal chair is chained to the floor and the other two are on the other side of the table and the fourth chair is back against the far wall as if it is the chair for the guard making sure the man in the chained chair doesn't do something crazy like bolt, fight, or drop or hide anything out of the view of the two in the other chairs. One marshal leads me to the chained chair and says, "Have a seat." Head then tells me, "We will be right back." I see Head smile at me and it's not like the smile he would give me on one of the nights we were out prowling for chicks. It seems to show too many teeth and there is a clear malevolence to it. The door slams shut. I wonder where they are observing me from. I don't know if it's a camera or a hidden mirror they are watching me from. I didn't wear my watch and so I soon become enamored in looking at the schoolhouse clock they have on the wall that is constantly clicking. Minutes become hours and soon I've been sitting there three hours. It's night by now. I know the building must be empty because straight up federal salaried employees aren't staying late except for those hardcore aggressive go-getter prosecutor types who want to conquer the world by tomorrow. Shit I can't do this. So this is putting someone on ice. No one offers me a drink or access to a bathroom. They want me deprived and twisted up so I'll be more susceptible to interrogation. Just as the clock ticks 8:30, I open my wallet. I look at the picture of my ex family and I say out loud I'm sorry y'all. I'm going to do whatever it takes to get back home to y'all and get back in your lives. I waste so much time and threw so much away for a nothing life.... Just at that instant Head and a new older marshal walk back in. Head is in his usual $2,000 suit, but not the same one he had on when they put me in this box. The marshal is in tactical gear with a nine millimeter slung low on his leg like a gunslinger with a black jumpsuit that says US Marshal across the front. He reaches his hand across to me with a dour look on his face. I'm Deputy Marshal Hagen. He has dark hair with gray fringe surrounding it. His mustache is salt and pepper. He is on the far side of fifty and his visage is hardened from probably seeing too much pain and suffering in his job. "I was in charge of the safety of Agent Johnson when he was testifying. As you can tell, we take safety of our witnesses paramount and in this case he was a brother agent"

"I'm sorry for your loss. But, I didn't have anything to do with it and I don't know anything about it."

Head reached over the table.

"JD, I'm not so sure. I think you lost your way a long time ago. Before you say a word, just know we have twenty seven tapes of you sniffing coke with agent Johnson and sleeping with his whores. One evening was a sting with you as the target because we have heard several allegations that you have been taking sex as a payment for legal representation." I'm floored. I can barely move I can't look up to meet his gaze.... "You passed that test that night but we still think you've been dirty ... look at yourself. Your suit is a mess. There are food stains on your shirt and grease stains on your tie. Your shoes are turned over and you almost never shave (by now a five o'clock shadow has arisen on my face and skull that I shaved this morning. We have seen you on tape having sex with hookers ... we have seen you at the strip clubs and paying hookers."

Agent Hagen starts in, "We don't care about your sex life. We care about the man you killed who left behind a wife and three kids."

"I didn't kill anybody or know anything about it," I protest. "I got to use the bathroom." I stand up to leave.

Head jumps up and shoves me down, "Fuck you punk! Piss down your pants leg. I trusted you. I thought you were a friend. I didn't know you are a cop killer. (Damn black cop showing out for the white. For the uninitiated, that means that a black police officer will be harsher on black defendants in front of white police officers so they will not mistake that officer for a homeboy or someone who gives a damn about any type of defendant.) Just then tears start to stream down my face. I, at least, thought I had my friend. My sex secrets are open to the world. How the hell did I think someday I could be a judge with the things I have done. With the time I have spent chasing hookers with the filth that I have wallowed in. And just like Head instructed, piss runs down my leg at just that moment. Head laughs an evil laugh.

"We got you bitch. How did your boy Billy pay you? We didn't see any major deposits in your account since you took this case. Yes, bitch we've been monitoring your money. Yeah, so was he paying you in women. So is that why you won't rat him out?" He walks to the door, gets a roll of paper towels, and throws them at me. "Clean that mess up and we will be back to talk to you." Hagen stands up, shakes his head and they both walk out and the door slams shut.

I'm not just scared. I'm cut to the bone. All of my secrets are out there. They have been investigating me. They are looking for a reason to put me in handcuffs. I take out my wallet and look at the picture of my ex family. Tears run down my face. My ex married me because she said she believed that I was a man that would protect and provide for her and her children and always make her laugh and here I sit the biggest joke of all. At that moment, the lowest in my life, I say a prayer. I pray for mercy not just for myself but also for my son who would have to live with the public knowledge that his father is a pervert and disbarred lawyer who is in jail. As I look at him and his mom, I make a resolve again. I'm coming home to you. And nothing is going to stop me from getting back home to my ex family. No, not ex, but my family. I clean myself up.

One or 2 hours later, Head and Hagen return. They plop down. Head is looking at me with laughter in his eyes. "Yo bro come on. Confession is good for the soul. Tell us what happened. I know Billy dragged you into this. You aren't no killer, you're just the bagman. Right. You provided the money and paid off the killer, right."

I look at Head and say, "Fuck you!" I want my lawyer. His name is Jeff Stephenson. His number is 410 777 9311. I invoke my right to counsel."

Head takes a Greater Baltimore Telephone book, puts it to the side of my face, and punches it with all his might. I see stars and momentarily go unconscious. I wake up lying on the floor with the book being repeatedly slammed on my face and body. All I can do is gag and I start to spit up blood. Mercifully what was probably 30 seconds of a beating stops and I drag myself up and stare at amazement at my former drinking buddy.

Head looks at me and says, "Bitch, you got no rights but what we give to you." He then drops the book to the floor, sits back in the chair, and looks at me straight in my face and laughs. "Big bad trial lawyer huh" You ain't shit. I got you Bitch." Just then Hagen gets a beep of his cell and picks it up. He then whispers furiously to Head. They look at each other and rush out of the room... and the door slams shut. Hours pass. I lie out on the floor and use my jacket for a pillow and look up at the naked bulb that has got to be the brightest damn bulb I have ever seen. It's so bright I can see it with my eyes closed so there is no reason to try to sleep. I can't. I put my head under my hands, and I think I really thought I was holding it together. I thought my life was a secret and I have made myself an open joke. What have I done to my life? I've thrown it all away? But you know what today I'm reborn. If they had all they said they had on me I would have been disbarred. I would have been locked up before now. What they have on tape is me refusing to do a representation for sex. That exonerates me from that issue. Today I'm reborn. I start to feel free even though I'm locked up in this box, because I don't have the burden of secrecy anymore. I'm laid bare and born anew. I'm going to be ok. At 6 am I'm lying there with a smile on my face. I have turned to my side and I'm lying on my side with the picture of my wife and son lying beside me. Slowly the door opens I look up and it's Head and Hagen. They say, "Get up Mr. Davis. You're free to go." Head looks sheepish. "Yo, JD bro. I knew you was innocent."

I just harrumphed, "So you found the real killer?"

"Yes it turns out Laquaana killed Jeremiah Johnson. It seems he had some secret accounts that he hid from our office where he had stored several hundred thousand dollars. He had them in Laquaana's name and given her the impression that he was going to take her with him after his testimony and move to the Caymans and have a happy life. Which she thought was true, until she found him in bed with the Little General". My mouth hit the floor. She actually killed them both but we aren't revealing the judge's death to the public. That was another reason you were our prime suspect. We thought the judge was the actual target and GrayBoy just got caught in some bullshit."

"How did you find all this out?"

"She was trying to fly to the Caymans with a suitcase full of cash and the straight razor she used on the judge in her luggage. It still had

115

his blood on it. If her simple ass hadn't tried to sneak a bag of weed through security, she would have gotten away, but when a drug-sniffing dog keyed on her luggage she was arrested. When we matched the blood, we told her she was facing the death penalty and she gave it up in exchange for a plea of life in prison. She's in a box just like this. Hagen walks away saying, "Good luck counselor," and he turns and stares straight at me and says "I'll catch you later."

Head and I are left there staring at each other. "I'm sorry JD. If I hadn't done what I did, they would have thought I was involved too. They know about my chasing just as they know about you."

"You let me piss on myself. You beat me."

"I'm sorry man."

"Fuck sorry, Head. It doesn't matter, but what you didn't know is that I've said goodbye to my whore chasing ways."

"Huh, what you talking 'bout nigga? You can't turn down no pussy. You can't turn nothing but your collar down. Nigga Please" and he laughs.

"No, Head. You see this picture I have of my wife and son. This is what I'm living for. This is what I can't turn down anymore. This is what I'm living for. I'm gonna go back to being the man I once was."

I brush past him. I hear him yell at my back, "Nigga you can't change. You and me. We the same nigga. I'll see you at Norma Jean's tomorrow nigga. Like always. Holla." He lights a cigar and walks away. I walk to the elevators and hit the ground button. As I exit, the security guard gets up and unlocks the door for me. I step out into a cool early Baltimore morning. The air is fresh and crisp and there is a little fog that a rising sun is starting to burn off. I take a lungful of air and breathe the breath of a free man. Hours ago I didn't know I would ever be free again and now I slowly turn up the hill toward the Mariner Arena and my home. Not home, but my apartment. My home is back in North Carolina with my wife and son. I walk into my building. I grab a bottle of Jack and walk back to the elevator and take it to the roof top deck and from my deck I watch the sun rise over the Inner Harbor for the first time in years. I take a deep drink off Jack that burns my throat and chest and I sit in a lounge chair and watch. That's where I fall asleep for my day's adventure is over. And tomorrow it's back to the drawing board and time to get ready for trial again.

CHAPTER 15

ANOTHER SATURDAY NIGHT AND
I AIN'T GOT NOBODY

I WAKE AT FIVE in the afternoon, still up on the rooftop of my condo building. I stretch and I look around. I'm the only one up there. Wow I camped out in Baltimore and nobody robbed me. I pick up my empty bottle of Jack and toss in the garbage can that is off to the far right of the roof. I walk down the steps enjoying the burn of the first exercise that I have had in a while. On my door is a note it has a red lipstick kiss on it and a slight hint of perfume. I open it up; it's from Carmen. She is essentially telling me how much she loved me and how much I hurt her and how can I not be the man she needs and depends on. How could I tell her lies...usually I would feel guilty about this but I realize I never told her any of those things? I can feel guilty about a lot of things in my life, but how can I be guilty for things I never did and I never told that woman I loved her. I crumple up the note and stumble inside my apartment. I walk over to my lazy boy and plop down. I open up my cell and stare at the picture of my family that had sustained me through so much. I see 37 missed calls from Carmen's number. I want to call, but I can't. Then I say fuck it. And I called the house. I hear a man's deep voice answer. What the fuck. My heart drops. I hear that voice say hello three times and it cracks a little but it's definitely a man's voice. I slam my phone shut and I sling it as hard as I can at the brick wall across the room. The phone shatters and I sit there with my hands in my face. She could have waited for me. She should have waited for me. She has another man so comfortable that he answers the phone in the house I paid for. The one I still pay for. My son is calling some other man Dad¼ Fuck that. I'll show her. I need some strange. Fuck all this. JD is back and on the prowl. Before I know it, I'm out the door and on my way to Norma Jeans. What about trial prep? Fuck trial prep. I just been through the damn grinder and found my way out. How could she get on with her life without me? I shake my head and push open the door to Norma Jeans five minutes later; I guess my own personal record.

The bartender gives me my usual. I grab a seat at the bar and start paying for one-dollar lap dances. A slim Puerto Rican honey comes up to me and says, "I know you. You're JD."

"Oh, am I famous? Where do you know me from? You used to date my girl Trina. She said you knew how to handle your business and you have a really nice crib just up the street."

Just then I get a nauseous feeling. Do I really want a bunch of strippers who are tied to criminals and drug dealers know where I lay my head? "I would love to see it some time." She hands me her number and I place it in my pocket. Five minutes later I head out. Man that was another reminder of where I had been. Look, I can go see some booties somewhere a little more socially acceptable and not so dangerous. I walk down the street and turn by the Stage Door nightclub and I walk into the Inner Harbor. I go into the main building on the right up the stairs and in twenty minutes I'm seated at a table with a bowl of delicious hot wings and fries in front of me with a beer at Hooters. I let my emotions take on those of the crowd who are raucously cheering for the Maryland Terrapins as they play the Duke Blue Devils. Duke. My wife is a journalism professor at Duke. I used to love to sit and see her work on an article with her feet tucked up under her and her hair hanging loose and a little frown on her face as she works on her story. Man it was all I could do to keep from ravishing her right on her desk with her story unwritten. Love will do that too you. Man, I even missed the little stories she would tell me about her day. I used to not appreciate the glances into her daily life. That was before I didn't get to hear them every day. There were a thousand things I missed. I missed her smile. I missed her interaction with my son, watching them laugh and play. I missed her head on my shoulder when she was contemplating life; her commentary on the importance of the first black president, and her excitement about me fueled me more than the other way around. Her constant encouragement to make me more successful and to make me a better man, I miss all that. Damn I must be the stupidest mutherfucker on earth. I left all of that for empty sex and drugs and money. Speaking of money I didn't have any ... my wife makes more than me, but she also gets the lion's share of my income which is what happens when you are at fault in a divorce because you are a stupid prick who can't control his dick. Man, none of these women I dealt with have the beauty and depth of my wife and I gave her up to be with them. My wife's last words were "I thought I had won when you married me but I can't compete for a man who is supposed to be all mine. I can't and I won't. Goodbye Jasper, goodbye". And she shut the door in my face. I take a deep gulp of my beer so deep that I start to choke and have to throw it up along with a gob of hot wings. Everyone turns to look at me but 'I'm damn near red from embarrassment. Now JD, the legendary Jack Daniels, can't even hold his liquor. I walk to the bathroom to clean myself up. After wiping the throw up off my shirt, I realize it's time to carry my black ass home. As I walk out, I see Carmen and three other beautiful exotic sisters sitting at the table with her. There is a pitcher of beer at the table. I freeze I don't know what to do. Their table is in laughter that abruptly stops as Carmen spots me. A look of pure hurt covers her face ,pain and betrayal. Her friends immediately ask her what's wrong. At that point I flee. Looking back I see a table full of angry black women staring at me. And the biggest and loudest of them yells, "Yeah, you better run you punk mutherfucka!" Man do I make a habit of hurting the women that actually care about me. As I slow to a jog and then a walk I head toward my condo. Why do I care more about the women who I know don't give a damn about me than I do about the ones who clearly love me and want me in their lives as a life mate? And I'm too drunk to deal with such deep nights and I stagger in to my apartment and for the third straight night I sleep by myself (The first night at my condo the second night in the lockup and the roof and now tonight stone drunk with droplets of throw up on me). But in my mind I feel it should not just be justified, but celebrated. I'm alone and not having sex. I know I got other issues, but I don't sniff cocaine anymore; I can't afford it. I drink, but all lawyers do that. It's justified since we deal with the problems of the world, so we are justified in drowning our sorrows... yeah, yeah, yeah. I flop on my bed with my mouth tasting like a science experiment from the mix of wing sauce, beer, and Jack. I sleep a deep dreamless sleep that seems to encompass the whole world in the fog of sleep.

CHAPTER 16

LET THE PEOPLE OF GOD SAY AMEN

I WAKE UP AT NINE am the next morning. It's Sunday and I'm determined to work on the trial but before I do I decide that I want to go see my Morehouse brother live and in person at his church, Power Temple. Let me go support brother Jamar. Maybe his words can provide the inspiration I need to get my life back on track and to go win my wife back. I change into my black closing suit, as there are always some pretty women in church. I'm looking sharp. For once, there is no food on my clothes and I take the time to shine my boots. There is a little grease on my tie but I decide that instead of changing ties, the grease stain makes me interesting and since it can't be seen when the tie is tucked inside the suit coat, it seems so trivial. I head out of the apartment and as I head out the door I notice I'm out of Jack, but I have Bacardi so I take a swig as I head out of the apartment and the burn feels good (to the uninitiated if you drink the same thing too much your body gets numb to it so you have to use other things to get the same high you used to get with other liquors, so I am feeling quite happy loosey goosey if you will, as I slip behind the wheel of my BMW 840 CI. I do a peel out as I head out of the garage and head to the Bolton Hill location of the church. Bolton Hill is a townhouse and mansion area of Baltimore. Beautiful old homes and mansions made of stone and slate but juxtaposed with drugged out hookers walking the street. But that's where Jamar chose to put his church, a beautiful place where the help of spirituality is needed. As I turn up McClellan Street, a Baltimore police cruiser pulls up behind me. Damn ,why did I drink half of the fifth of Bacardi? I must stink to high hell of liquor. Damn, I see visions of East Eager Street (the Baltimore city jail). After five minutes, they pull up beside me, wave and keep going. I almost throw up with the amount of stress I was under. Man, maybe I have a drinking problem, too. Can it be more than the women? Maybe I'm codependent. Maybe I'm just an addictive person and the very next thought is "Man, I could really use a beer and a lap dance right about now.".... At about that same time, I pull up to the Empowerment Temple. I park my car beside some of the most extravagant cars in Baltimore. My 840 are neighbors with a Lexus LS 400 and a Mercedes S600. That's Jamar's church. The most affluent and the poorest rub elbows and sing praises together here. And right now I'm definitely one of Baltimore's unfortunate, but yet I'm fortunate to be free. I try to put a good face on as I go. It's hard to keep my eyes off all the swaying backsides that I see as I approach the church's front door. There are beautiful sisters of every shade and some gorgeous white girls too and they all love the lord Jesus. Maybe I should have come to church earlier. I immediately put those thoughts out of my head. I bend my head and praise God for without him my ass would be heading to the city jail for drunk driving or better yet heading to federal prison for the murder of a judge and an undercover DEA agent. I have a lot to pray about. As the music plays and people shout and rejoice, I'm waiting for the word. As Jamar comes out, he has a message about coveting and how we covet what we see and how what we covet is not ours and because we are so busy coveting we can't see what we have and what God has given us because we are so busy desiring what others have. The message hit me like a sledgehammer. I had a beautiful wife and son and I coveted the lifestyle of single men chasing woman and gave away my God given gift of a perfect wife for bimbos. Tears well up in my eyes. I step up to the altar and pledge to recommit my life to Christ... I am contrite. I'm sad and happy all at the same time. As I walk out of the church, I'm oblivious to all around me and think only about what that message meant to me. I hop in my car and zip over to the office. It seems deserted. I walk to my office and pull up my computer file on Billy Badass... I have his file linked to his close associates and girlfriend Laquaana who always has issues in family court with her three other baby daddies which I handled for her because of Billy.... As I'm reviewing her files to see how I can use her arrest to Billy's favor, in walks Jeff and he has a troubled look on his face. "Hey JD, We need to talk."

"What's up Jeff?"

Jeff shuts the door and sits on the left corner of our desk. "JD, we can't work as partners anymore."

"Oh, I see now that a brother is down."

"JD, nobody made you make a mess of your life like you did. Nobody made you leave your family. Nobody made you sleep with whores and our support staff. You're out of control and I'm not going to lose my livelihood and family like you have because of your shenanigans. Your problems aren't gonna ruin my life, do you understand? I'm not your little buddy from high school. I'm not Gilligan and you aren't the Skipper."

I sit quietly for three minutes while Jeff rants and raves and blows off steam. "Jeff, I've come to grips with a lot of what you have said today and I've implemented a plan to change my life."

"Like what."

"I called all my sex partners and I've told them it's over."

Jeff looks at me incredulously. "Bullshit"

"No brotha. JD is hanging up his boots. I'm gonna get my family back and my life and my sanity."

"Oh, yeah. Ok, if you really changed JD open the third drawer on the left side of the desk.... (That's where I keep my condoms and my whiskey." I open the drawer. Jeff takes a garbage bag from the hallway and dumps the three full pints and 30 Trojan Magnum condoms in the gold wrapper in the garbage can. I wince and say thank you. That's just helped me."

He says, "Ok give me the bottle in your overcoat hanging behind the door as well." I wince and get up and it joins the other bottles with a clinking sound. "And now give me the half pint in the plant by the window."

I gulp and say, "You know about that one too, huh?" I go over and that bottle joins the others and I hear the sound of glass shattering as it hits the previous bottles.

"JD if you can do this, I'm on your side, brotha." and Jeff turns to walk out.

I yell, "Wait!" and as he turns back with the wastebasket in his hand, I open up my briefcase and I drop out 7 of the nine miniature Jack Daniels bottles I have in there in the garbage. Jeff raises his eyes in surprise (I couldn't give him all I still gotta prep for trial and it will be at least an hour until I get home and can access my bottles at home). I decide right then that after I finish these two miniatures I won't drink anymore in the office. That will just be off limits. As Jeff shakes his head and walks out, I quickly throw the two miniatures down my gullet one after the other. Boy I needed that. As the liquor settles in my stomach, I look at the computer files and try to figure out what to do. Then I realize what I can do. I see an opening and tomorrow I will take it. I power down and leave the office. I wave at Jeff as I walk by. He still shakes his head as he works on whatever corporate deal he has hopping. Man I can't imagine life without Jeff. He has been my best friend when I wasn't even my own friend. I got to do him proud.

I walk back to the condo. This is now my fourth day sleeping by myself. I feel like I'm going to erupt like a volcano if I don't have some intimacy soon, but I've made a change and I know if I backslide I will fall all the way back into my morass of sex and death...I walk into my apartment and flop into my chair and recline back and I fall asleep with my Sirius radio on channel 51 with smooth R and B.

CHAPTER 17

And by decision, the winner is....

I WAKE UP AT 7:30 and realize I didn't have any Jack last night because I went to sleep before I took my daily sip. So I could either start this as the first day of sobriety just like it's my fifth day of chastity. I just don't know if it's wise to go cold turkey in the middle of a trial. So discretion is the better part of valor, so I took a fresh bottle of Jack and broke the seal, and took a deep swig and man that burn will wake you up in the morning. I feel a little woozy as the Jack hits my head and I stumble to the closet. On the way I trip over my pants from last night and fall backwards and hit my head on the floor, as I lay there I look up at the spinning ceiling fan and think maybe Jack for breakfast isn't the best thing in a world. I get my ass up. I walk to the sink and pour the rest of the Jack down the sink. The smell of it is so strong; I actually got nauseous from the smell of it. Hey maybe my body is rejecting the liquor and it will fight it off for me. Made happy by the thought, I get dressed in a clean navy blue suit from Brooks Brothers. I slip on my trial boots, grab my bag, and I'm out the door. It's a cool brisk morning and I walk quickly to the courthouse. As I set up at my trial table, I notice that there are significantly more people in the courtroom. The gallery is packed with media and onlookers. I guess the case has got more interesting since GrayBoy was murdered and the Little General had his throat slit. (To the uninitiated, when there is a black man killing another black man you have an empty courtroom like we have had in this case for the last two weeks, but when you mix in the murder of whites all of a sudden the media cares and shows up and the courtroom is packed.) So as I scan the courtroom, I stop on the far right corner, and there I see Carmen sitting there with a somber look on her face. She stands up and motions for me to come to her and she heads to the door. Not awaiting my response. I look at the clock and see that there is still fifteen minutes before court is to start, so I gird my loins and I walk towards the door as I leave the protection of the courtroom. The media surge towards me and follow me out the door. I see Carmen walk into the lawyers lounge and I use my electric passkey and then turn around and have to force the door closed in the face of an extra persistent TV reporter. As I turn around, I see Carmen perched on the end of the long table in the lounge. Her face is impassive; her arms are crossed. She is looking deadly and lovely in her immaculate red suite with white silk blouse and three inch heels on her feet. This woman is so magnificent.

"Jasper, you hurt me. No one is allowed to hurt me."

I stutter, "I didn't mean to. I was just..."

"You were just trying to treat me like a whore."

"Like a whore? We never slept together. We barely kissed. I treated you like a princess. I put you on a pedestal," I yelled.

She stands up, "Don't you dare raise your voice to me? You don't have the right. You sucked me in with words and protestations of love. You had me open up to you, my deepest darkest secrets and when I'm at my most vulnerable you don't comfort me and love me and hold me. You reject me over a phone call. You're a callous, uncaring asshole. I won't allow you to hurt me." With that she reaches back with her left hand and comes across my face. Wow, did she have a brick in her hand? I see stars and little birdies like you see in a Bugs Bunny cartoon. As I recover, I see a glistening in her eyes behind her wire-rimmed glasses. Streams of tears roll down her cheek. "You don't have the right to hurt me or anyone else. I know that you don't want to be a slut anymore but you don't get to treat me like my ex did, like I'm a woman on a pedestal, too good to touch, but not too good to cheat on. I demand respect. Whether you love me or not, you will respect me. I demand that of a man. JD, grow up and learn how to love more of a woman than her body." I hang my head in shame. "Just stay away from me JD". (This is the first time she ever used my nickname and I've never heard it used with more venom than that ever before in my life). She walked out and slammed the door. I slump onto the green micro fiber sofa against the wall. Wow, for a little woman, she packs a real punch. I look at the clock on the wall and "Oh, shit!" It's 45 seconds before the judge takes the bench. I grab the table and pull myself off the sofa. As I walk to the door, I notice the beginning of a painful looking black eye. Thanks Carmen. It will look great in front of the jury. The minute I walk into the courtroom, Judge P. takes one look at me and shakes his head and beckons both Yao and me to the bench.

"Mr. Davis, you are looking as if you are the dictionary definition of disreputable. Your worn out suit, your run over shoes, and now your face looks like you have been in a street fight". He then raises his nose and takes a sniff and miracles of miracles "At least I don't detect any odor of alcohol from you so I guess you're ready for trial, counselor".

With a grimace, "Ok, ok I'm ready your honor." Yao smirks. It's not a mean smirk but the self-satisfied smirk they issue to all prosecutors when they start that job (I think I lost mine in a poker game... just remember a straight beats three of a kind especially if the holder of the straight is holding a straight tire iron at the time). We both walk back to our respective seats. And the judge says, "I will now hear arguments on the previous application from Friday from the prosecution in regards to a potential mistrial... Mr. Yao. Please proceed."

"Thank you, your Honor" Yao says as he rises to his feet. "Your honor, a mistrial is a necessity in this case. A sworn witness, who has been introduced to the jury whom I talked about in opening statements, has been murdered and our evidence shows that the murderer is the girlfriend of the defendant. It is our position that since the defendant through his girlfriend had a part in this murder, he should not be able to gain from his acts by being protected by double jeopardy attaching."

Judge P. harrumphs, "Counselor haven't you had several witnesses that gave direct eyewitness testimony as to what the defendant has been alleged to have done. Is there anything that the dead DEA agent could have added to that?"

"Yes your honor. He could have testified as to the general lawlessness of this defendant and how this defendant was dangerous and other prior acts of violence of this defendant.

I assert your honor; we have not been given any notice of any prior violence that the prosecution wanted to introduce. Mr. Davis do you have argument?"

"Yes I do, your honor. The prosecution has left out crucial facts in the argument. Now your honor, it is true that a defendant cannot and should not gain immunity from prosecution though double jeopardy if the mistrial is caused through his own bad acts. There is no connection between any bad acts of my client. Your honor it is asserted by the prosecution that my client had a part in the murder of the witness, but I myself was present Saturday night and early Sunday morning when the murderess was arrested and it was clear that neither my client nor I, as Mr. Yao asserted, had anything to do with this murder. The allegation the US Marshal service briefed me is that the murder took place because GrayBoy aka Jeremiah Johnson and the Little General were lovers and Laquaana Richardson, my client's ex-girlfriend, that GrayBoy was not gonna run off with her, but with the little Judge, and when she found that out she murdered them both." The judge raises both eyebrows and there is a visible and audible gasp from the peanut gallery. The chattering of people goes from a mist to a small roar to a sea of cacophony. Judge P. in a flash brings down his gavel and says, "Order!" the deputy says out loud "If there is another outburst like that, we will clear this courtroom immediately.

"Mr. Yao, is there any truth to what Mr. Davis says?"

Yao says, "I never heard any of that."

I immediately rise up out of my chair and say, "Mr. Buncombe (Head) can verify what I have said as well."

Yao stares daggers at Head who sheepishly says, " What Mr. Davis says is true. I didn't tell Mr. Yao this, but yes its true." Reporters stream out of their chairs and head to the exit doors to feed this wild ass story to every cable outlet and news media on the planet.

The judge glares at Mr. Yao. "Counselor, you dare stand up in this courtroom and tell me a false hood. Stand up man, and take your medicine."

Yao drags himself to his feet by the table and just then, even though he isn't anywhere near me, his sphincter releases and I gag. Jesus, what the fuck has he been eating? The Judge then proceeds to ream every last bit of honor, decorum, and dignity out of Yao through his ass. And when he finishes, his last words are "Motion denied. Call your next witness. Bring in the jury and, Mr. Yao, if you breathe a word of this to the jury, you'll spend the rest of your legal career begging bar counsel to restore your license, but they won't because it will be hanging over the mantle of my fireplace. Do we understand each other?"

With a barely audible gasp slash whisper, Yao says "Yes."

Judge P. says, "I can't hear you, counsel. I can only hear words if they are followed with 'yes judge' or 'yes your honor.' So which is it?"

"Yes your honor, Sir. I'm ready to proceed."

I keep a somber face so Judge P. won't turn on me. My client looks at me and says, " Dude, you the best lawyer on the East Coast. When this trial is over, I'm going to give you a big bonus."

I reply, "I can't accept a bonus under the Professional Rules of Responsibility, but tell your friends JD is the mutherfucka. You thought I was play pimpin' didn't you?

"Bet. Man show you right you. Damn right, I will", Billy replied.

As the jury enters, you can visibly see that Yao's spirit has been broken. He stutters through a simple "the people rest."

Judge P. turns to me and says "Is there any evidence from the defendant?" I turn and look at the clock at the back of the wall and see it's already 1 o'clock. "Your honor, I didn't expect the prosecution to end its case so quickly."

"Neither did I, Mr. Davis," the judge quips.

"I'd request that we restart tomorrow and that tomorrow we will either have our closings or I will call my first witness."

"That's fine. Court is adjourned," and the judge admonishes the jury "do not watch any media tonight or while this case is pending. Do not watch or read any accounts of this case on TV, in the newspaper or any electronic media, which means blogs, as well as Twitter, Facebook, and anything that may comment on this case. That is the only way to fairly ensure that both the defendant and state receive a fair trial. Have a good evening and I'll see you at 9:30 am. Good day."

As the deputy says, "All rise," the judge strides out. The jury walks out and Yao and Head slink out. Head looks at me with pleading eyes. I just notice at that point that my eye is stinging. I touch it and a lance of pain goes through me. As the media that have waited on me block the aisle, I simply put my bag on and start shoving my way through, pushing different media members to the floor and at least two women. As I shove my way out the door, I pause and someone walks by my closed right eye but I can't make him or her out. The next thing I notice out of my left eye, it's Carmen. She cradles my face with her hands. "Poor little JD. Did I do that to you?"

I said, "No, it was Mike Tyson and Smoking Joe Frazier."

"Well, I'm sorry JD. She pulls my face close and kisses my forehead.

I say, "Carmen, I can't do this. I gotta work and you've made it clear that you don't feel for me." Then a sharp stinging hand comes across my face and, damn, she hit me in my left eye, too.

"Fine, suit yourself asshole." Now the left eye starts to swell. Great, now I look like a raccoon. I got to get home while I can still see. I rush out the door and I only bump into five people on my way to my condo. As I hit the front door, out pops Jenny the taller of my two Asian fantasy girls.

"JD, are you ok? Who beat you up, honey? Oh, I'm so sorry. Let me help you to your room." She takes my hand and leads me to the elevator as we reach what I can only assume is our floor, she leads me to the door I think is mine but hey she didn't take my key. Oh, shit she didn't need my key to lead me into my place. She took me to her place. She yells out to her friend "hey, look what I found" and she shoves me onto her sofa. I fall back and the next thing I know I feel two bodies crawl on me. As it happens, I feel tears run down my eyes. I have no control over my life and now I have no control over my body. "JD, what's wrong? Why are you crying?"

"I just want to go home to my wife. I mean my ex-wife. I want to remain celibate. I can't do this anymore."

"Wow JD. I thought we had fun together."

"Ladies it isn't fun for me anymore. I want to be happy again. I look like a blind palooka."

"JD, we thought you liked to have fun. What's this? Tears are definitely not sexy. You know what. Get out. We don't ever want to see you again."

"See me again? I can't see you now. I can't find my way to my apartment." I feel two little hands grab me and pull me to my feet with my pants still down around my ankles and they are surprisingly strong as they yank me out of the apartment which due to me unluckiness, I just happen to be close enough for the door to hit my nose and the crisp crack I hear tells me it's broken. Plus the sharp pulsing pain I immediately feel. And I thought this was going to be a good day. Why is everything so good in the court house, but so bad in real life? As I struggle to pull my pants up, I catch a little glimpse through my swollen eyes of Javon the building maintenance guy. I say " Yo Javon, help a brother out."

"Help you out. Bro, it's not going down like that. You in the hallway with your pants half down, your dick hard as a rock, looking like you been in a knock down drag out street fight and you want my help? Sheeeyyyyyiiit."

"No, just point me towards my door. I have had the most fucked up day in existence."

I feel him grab my shoulders, orient me to the left, and say, "take about twenty good steps and then turn right and you will be at your door."

As I struggle with my pants now up, but unbuttoned and unbelted, I walk in the dark towards my door. After feeling the wall for 12 minutes, I find my door and find my key by touch. I walk over to my easy chair and collapse (I've done the same thing so many times, I don't need to see to be able to do this...I feel on the floor by my right side and there is an already open bottle of Jack Daniels. My eyes are so swollen that I have to slide the bottle across my face to my mouth to take a drink and unlike every other time I drink Jack, I don't get a sweet burn. I gag and choke as it goes down the wrong pipe. Shit. I go into uncontrollable coughing. Man, how can I fall any further? Jack can't give me any comfort. It burns my nostrils and I cough so much I become hoarse. As the coughing subsides, I feel like reality drops on me like a ton of bricks. I can't continue to do the same thing and expect different results. I believe that is what Einstein says is the definition of insanity. I've been insane for at least ten years of my life. Tears rain down my face and I sit back in my chair. Every time I try to rub my eye, it hurts from the swelling and the coughing exacerbates the pain in my nose as well. At this point, I'm a mess of Jack and snot and tears, and a trickle of blood is running down my face. Enough is enough. It's time for me to change my life. I take a deep breath, pick up the Jack bottle, walk to my kitchen sink, and I pour it down the sink. And I'll be dammed if my eyesight doesn't get a little better. Can this be real? I walk to my utility closet and I pull out the ten unopened pint-size bottles of Jack I have stored in there and I methodically pour them down the sink. As I do this, a calm comes over me that I haven't felt in a lot of years. At this point I know I can do what I never thought I could. I can walk away from Jack Daniels and alcohol in general. As peace and serenity comes over me, suddenly I'm so very tired that I lie down and go to sleep and for the first time in years I feel a glow in my inside that is not the direct result of liquor being ingested by me or by the proximity of a woman to me. I'm happy and comfortable in my own skin and sober. I look at my watch it is 6:30 p.m. and I go to sleep and sleep the rest of night and for once I'm free.

CHAPTER 18

Decision day: Does he testify?

I WAKE UP THE next morning at 6:30 a.m. and I know this because my silver Kenneth Cole chronograph is still on my arm. I had slept for exactly twelve hours ... I take a yawn and stretch that lasts forever. And I feel soooo good. The swelling has gone down on my eyes, so I have decent vision. As I shuffle to the bathroom for my morning piss, I pull down my shorts and let out a torrent of piss that is strong enough to drown a fish... as the piss burns out of me I catch a glimpse of myself in the mirror. I look like a raccoon from the swelling around my eyes and nose but for the first time in a long time I see a discernible smile on my face and seeing that makes me smile even wider... as the last drop trickles out. I reel the one eyed monster back in and pull my shorts up. I walk over to the mirror and sink and I look myself in the eyes. Superficially I look like a raccoon, but there is a confidence that I haven't seen in many a moon. I don't see lust and avarice... I don't see liquor muscles. I see the practiced eye of a skilled trial lawyer no matter how black the circle that encircles those eyes is. No, I am not just a damn trial lawyer. I'm a human being, not a tool, but a person. I'm a person. I'm Jasper Davis, a father, an ex-husband, a man who used to volunteer to coach his son's baseball teams and cheered at my son's basketball games. I used to be a man who my wife could lean on and depend on... that's who I see glimmers of now. I feel confident then I immediately sag because while I may know I'm different no one else will. They will see as Judge P. put it the definition of a disreputable ass lawyer in a beat up suit, dirty clothes, and with black eyes and a broken nose and eyes that are chronically red from the drink and late nights...I know I'm different now I just have to prove to other people I'm different. I look at the clock its eight o'clock. I take out my razor and foam up my face and head and I shave for the first time since I went out with Carmen, but for the first time I do in a long time I do it because I want to feel good about myself not because I want to impress someone about how chic and suave I am. I slap some old school Old Spice on my face and I inhale the musky smell. I love and feel the burn of where I have nicked myself, but it doesn't hurt me it warms me. I walk out of the bathroom and head towards my wardrobe. I look in my chest of drawers and lo and behold I find a white Kenneth Cole non-iron shirt that is still in its wrapper. I smile, open it up, and withdraw all the pins and cardboard and the plastic of its wrapper. I walk over to my drawer and I throw it in on high. I walk back to my closet and there hung up is the black suit I wore when I went out with Carmen, and unlike the rest of my suits it isn't smeared with food or liquor stained or cum stains on the lap of the pants. I grab the shirt out of the dryer, which is still warm to the touch. I put it on and then immediately put my pants on and slip on my boots. I can be perfect and I am freeballing with no drawers on, but outwardly I look fresher and sharper that I have in a longtime. I throw on my jacket and grab my beat-up black trial bag and I scoop my laptop off of my dining table where I had left it and I head for the door. I have to be early today to discuss with Billy if he intends to testify. As I walk to the outside, a bright sun greets. Man, it's so bright that it makes me squint my bruised eyes, which give me a pretty good twinge of pain. I put my right hand over my eyes to shield my eyes from the glare. Wow what has got into the world today? I then promptly take off for the courthouse. Man, the sun feels so good on my skin it is like I'm being held in the palm of God's hands. As I walk up to Clarence Mitchell Courthouse, I start to feel an involuntary twitch in my face. I get the shakes and damn it I'm nervous. I don't think I'm nervous because I'm on trial. I think I'm nervous because I know what my time and exposure to the insipid life of a major felony trial lawyer is the place where blackness has seeped into my soul... this is the place of my fall and the potential place of my demise. As I stand there, I feel the

135

glow of the sun warming my spirit and right then think of the Twenty Third Psalm...instead of rap music that is my theme music now. Yea though I walk through the shadow of death, I shall fear no evil for thou art with me. Thy rod and staff comfort me and maketh a place for me beside cool waters and restoreth my soul surely goodness and mercy shall follow me all the days of my life and I shall dwell in the house of the lord forever. As I go up the steps, my legs stop quacking with every step. My back is more erect; my spirit is stronger. As I walk into the courthouse I flash my green card and check my watch and see it's 8:15 a.m. I head to the lockup and ask the corrections officers for permission to speak with my client William Johnson... they say ok and walk me to a small enclosed area covered with a chain link fence inside the locked dungeon of the corrections pen inside the courthouse. I grab a seat on one of the rusty looking metal chairs. I have to balance myself because I feel like one of the legs are loose and can give way at any moment (pretty much the same way I feel about myself right now as well). I hold it together and do my chair-balancing act and in 15 minutes Billy is shown into the room and he sits in the other chair, which outwardly seems to be much better balanced than mine.

As soon as Billy sits Down I say, "It's time Billy."

Billy asks, "Time for what? What you talking 'bout JD?"

"Billy it's time for you to decide if you want to testify"

"You my lawyer," Billy retorted. "You tell me what to do and what to say so I can go home." Billy is actually looking cross-eyed at me as well at this time.

"Well Mr. Johnson, the decisions and right to testify lie totally with the individual defendant. I cannot make that decision for you. Only you can make that determination."

As I stand there, I feel myself being searched by Billy's eyes as if the answer is somewhere on my face and if he searches enough he will read it on my skin and he will read it off to me. "Billy, in the United States every defendant has the right to testify. You have the right to tell your story and no one including me can take that right away from you."

"Well, what should I do?"

"My advice is that you don't testify. If you testify your whole record will be laid out in front of the jury: your prior assaults, your prior strong-arm robberies. Look, this is Baltimore. Nowhere else can a jury be handed what appears to be an air tight case and the jury rejects it, because they don't like the police or witnesses. The prosecution brings it and I think the DEA has given me the way to discredit the whole damn case

"JD, my life is in your hands brotha... you know other mutherfuckers told me you were a horny ass drunk and not to leave my life in your hands, but I can see now you are the right man for the job go get 'em son."

I glance at my watch and notice it's now a quarter 'til and I need to get in the courtroom ... "see you upstairs."

"Yo JD can you give me some smokes like you did last week at the jail. I'm fiendin' like a mutherfucka."

"I can't do that, Billy. It's against the rules, against the law and I can't do something like that."

"What? What the fuck did you mean by that? Yo. You did it before."

"Billy do you want smokes or do you want to go free. Let me do that for you. Let me focus on fighting for you and not on some damn cigarettes."

"Ok, ok. JD do your thing."

I turn my back on Billy and ring the buzzer for the guard. I don't even turn around and look at him which probably is maddening for Billy. I'm not sure how many people have chastised Billy Badass then turn their back on him. But I did and thirty seconds later the officer opens the conference room. I look back at Billy he isn't mad, he isn't raging; he's just looking at me curiously trying to figure it all out. JD had just said no to him while locked in a cage with him. I leave the correction's pens and head up to the courtroom three floors above the pens. As I hit the courtroom door, I see the room is once again packed to the gills. I walk to my trial table. As I sit my stuff down, I survey the courtroom. I see

Carmen in the back corner again. I hold her gaze for a minute and shake my head and turn away... no one is gonna throw me off my game today. Head makes a big show of coming over and saying, "What's shaking JD?" We missed you at Norma Jeans last night"

I stand fully erect and look Head directly in the eye. "I'm over that place, Detective Buncombe and I'm over our friendship. Don't touch me again," I say as I remove his hand from my back." Don't ever talk to me again outside of business." I then stage a whisper "house nigga run back to your massa". Head's face falls to the ground. He walks back over to Yao and the Judge strides into the courtroom. The deputy intones, "All rise" as the judge waves it off and says, "Be seated. Counselors. Mr. Davis nice suit. I can see your face still shows the results of your street fight from yesterday, but you look less disreputable than you did yesterday." I then move for a directed verdict, since the prosecution has rested. I don't believe even construing the facts most favorably to the prosecution a reasonable jury could not find my client guilty beyond a reasonable doubt on the evidence it has before them. He offhandedly says, "Motion denied. Anything else?"

"No your honor. I'm ready to proceed." He starts to say something to me that looks like it's a smart remark and I stare him down. I look at him emotionlessly. He holds my gaze for a full thirty seconds. The silence is deafening but I refuse to break his gaze or turn away from him. I'm gonna stand my ground. Judge P. then intones, "So bring in the jury."... The jury shuffles in and the Judge turns to me. Mr. Davis please call your first witness. The defense calls Laquaana Richardson... Yao jumps up sputtering your honor may we be heard??? The judge frowns and motions us up to the bench.. Your honor Mrs. Richardson already testified if Mr. Davis had any questions he could have asked her when she was on the stand before. Judge P. turns to me. I calmly state,

"Just as I don't control the prosecution's case and the witnesses they call. They don't control my case. I have a right to call any witness I deem appropriate, and if the court will look at the witness list, which I submitted two weeks prior to trial you will see Ms. Richardson is a listed witness. I would ask the court its assistance in compelling the prosecution to produce Ms. Richardson who is a guest of the federal government to bring her into court"...

Yao fumes, "Judge, this is outrageous". Judge P. looks at Yao

"Shut up counselor. Deal with it. If this witness is in custody in Baltimore, I expect her in this court in thirty minutes"... Do you have any other witnesses, Mr. Davis, while we wait? "No your honor, but I would invite the court to use this time to inquire of my client if he would choose to testify or whether he waives his right to do the same".

"That's fine. Step back counsels. Yao walks back with bad posture looking hangdog, maybe somebody should explain to these prosecutors and show how important body language is to their cause and how it can affect a jury's perception of them. Oh well, I'm damn sure not gonna tell him while I'm fighting it out with him at trial. As we reach the tables, the judge tells the jury we have a few matters that must be taken care of out of your presence, so if you could return to the jury room. There is audible grumbling from the jury which has up until this point been out of their lives and in court for two weeks now and to them there is no visible end in sight. So I'm sure that after two weeks of prosecution witnesses, they will reward me when I rest my case today. He heheheh. As the door to the jury room closes, the judge looks directly at my client and says.

"Mr. Billy Bada---- I mean Mr. William Johnson will you please rise ? Billy does so slowly and nervously(it's amazing how the toughest thug shakes like loose booty meat when they are in court and addressing a judge).

"Yes, your honor", his voice breaks like a teenager going through puberty.

"Sir you do understand that it is your absolute right to testify on your own behalf?"

"Yes, sir."

"And do you understand it is your decision alone not your lawyer's nor mine nor anyone else's to do so. You have the right to make the determination of whether you testify or not do you understand?"

"Yes, sir."

"Have you consulted with your attorney and do you believe you fully understand your right to testify?"

"I'm not sure, your honor."

"Well take a moment and speak to your attorney to make sure ."

"Thank you, Judge P." Billy leans towards me.(I fucking hate it when you spend time after time with a client explaining to them there rights to do anything, but when they get in front of a judge they act like you didn't tell them shit. That's one of my fucking pet peeves. I hope my frustration isn't showing on my face.

"What's your question, Billy ?"

"Are you telling me I can't testify?"

"No, Billy I'm not telling you that. As the judge said, that is your decision. I'm advising you not to testify, but it's all in your hands. If you testify, the prosecutor can ask you not only about your prior convictions but prior bad acts. You can't say you were somewhere else because no alibi notice was filed because you never told me you had an alibi (i.e. proof that you were somewhere else when the murder took place). Without that, you'll have to admit you were there which will put you on the scene. Right now, they have the testimony of witnesses who either have or appear to have a motive to lie."

"But it would be better if I denied I did this shit right?"

"Yes, but you can't just deny it and walk away. The prosecutor gets to ask you pretty much what they want to. My advice is don't do it.

"You know what JD? You underestimate me I have a good mouthpiece. If it wasn't for my mouthpiece how do you think I've been able to operate without getting hemmed up without getting turned out. This jury likes me and that little white girl who is juror ten has been digging on me . If I turn this mother out, not only will she vote not guilty, but she will be in my bed the same night."

"Goddamn arrogance. Why do people think they can always talk their way out of shit? You can't Billy , if you get caught in a lie and you're done."

Just then a little Spanish girl in a short Catholic school getup walks up to Yao and hands him a note and Yao asks to approach. As we approach, I'm steaming at my dumbass client who is about to throw away all the hard work I have done in setting this case up for reasonable doubt and my gambit with Laquaana will be for nothing. When we reach the bench, Yao tells the Judge that the US Marshals have Laquaana just outside the courtroom doors and are anxious to return her to the federal lock up and if this can be accommodated they would greatly appreciate it.

Judge P. replies, "Well I'm always ready to accommodate the US government. Step back. Are you ready to call your witness? We can continue the inquiry after this testimony."

"Yes, your honor," I replied. I'm still fuming at Billy who is sitting there with his arms crossed and a pout on his face like a little bitch. Why do people always think they can talk their way out of shit? As I reach my trial table, the jury files in again and the judge asks me, "Mr. Davis, please call your first witness."

"Your honor, the defense calls Laquaana Richardson. "And I turn to look at the main courtroom doors. As they open, I see Laquaana Richardson walk in escorted by two burly female US Marshals. None of the arrogance she had before is apparent. She is like a sail with the wind lost and shredded down the middle completely listless. As she shuffles her way to the witness stand, I steal a glance at the jury. I see their amazement at seeing the same confident woman they saw before broken down. As she takes her seat, the judge tells her

"Ms. Richardson, you are still under oath do you understand?"

Laquaana replies meekly," Yes, your honor"

"Good afternoon, Ms. Richardson," I say after I take a glance at my Kenneth Cole watch. "Good afternoon JD."

"Ms. Richardson, I would much prefer if you would address me as Mr. Davis just as I give you the courtesy of calling you Ms. Richardson." Yao jumps up and objects.

Judge P. looks at Yao incredulously, "You are going to object to the upholding of courtroom decorum? Counselor, really you have been a lawyer too long to make such frivolous objections. Sit down." And Yao flows drops like a balloon in which the helium is leaking out quickly and holds his face in his hands looking down and shaking his head. I then say, "Ms. Richardson, can you do me that courtesy I ask?"

She says, "Yes, Mr. Davis with a slight frown on her face (it's the ghetto girl attitude coming back).

"Ms. Richardson, the last time you came her you were dressed in a rather nice frock??"

"Frog? What is that Mr. Davis I don't wear no damn frog"

"Not Frog, Ms. Richardson. Frock as in dress?"

"Oh, yeah ok I'm following you now". She leans forward in the chair as if to pay close attention to what I'm saying.

"Today you are wearing a blue jumpsuit. Before, you walked in under your own power and today you are escorted by the US Marshals. What is the change in your circumstances?"

"I uh got arrested for some little shit stuff. I mean stuff. Little stuff yeah you know this or that. Little stuff." I can see Yao dying a thousand deaths in his chair to the left of me.

"So you call the murder of a federal agent and a state court judge a little something?"

"Yeah but it was over some street shit. Dude was supposed to love me but he was on the down low with this faggot. Instead of being with me, he chose to be with the sissy. So I had to get them JD..I mean Mr. Davis. It's the code of the streets right. If I didn't, no one would respect me. I gave up my baby" (pointing to the table where Billy was at) to be with a lying white faggot who used me".

"What was the street name of your lover?" "They called him Mr. GrayBoy, but the feds told me his name is Jeremiah Johnson. I look at the jury and see their eyes in shock and mouths drop to the floor as they place the name with the clean shaven agent who had been on the stand before them.

Yao jumps up and says," Objection your honor. This has nothing to do with the case at hand, the murder of Linwood White".

Judge P. looks at me and says, "Mr. Davis, what say you?"

"I'm about to link this all up if I could have the court's brief indulgence. "

"Well, be quick about it Mr. Davis."

I turn to Laquaana. "Ms. Richardson. What was your relationship with Mr. Johnson aka GrayBoy?"

"Well after I left Billy, the man who really loved me, I went to GrayBoy cause he told me he had a million dollars and we was gonna run away to Switzerland and we were gonna have a good life." Yao Jumps up and says, "Your honor... "

Judge P. turns to me and says "Move it along, Mr. Davis"

"Ms. Richardson did you ever talk to Mr. GrayBoy in regards to this case?"

"Yes, I did."

"What did he tell you?"

"He told me to tell the court that I saw Billy kill that Linwood dude. He said it was what would free us to move on because he wouldn't have to look over his back wondering if Billy was looking for us. So I came in to court and said what I said." I look at Laquanna 's face for tells (little indications she's lying). I don't see any. I don't hear any stress in her voice. She is talking plaintively and matter of factly. She knows that all pretense is gone and her life is over. Her only hope is that Billy may have some pity on her and put some money in her commissary every once in a while. Or maybe visit her in prison. That's hard to know that that all your life boils down to at the age of 28, but it's all she has left. I'm left with a choice, just because she testified that she was told to testify by GrayBoy it doesn't mean that she didn't see Billy stomp Linwood. Now in my gut I know that Billy did this. So I don't ask the ultimate question, because I believe I have enough taint on this case to make the jury doubt it, especially a Baltimore jury. I tell the judge I have no further questions for this witness. As I look at Yao, I see him spring to his feet and he literally cannot wait to get at this witness.

"Ms. Richardson you realize you are under oath?"

"Correct."

"And you realize you have sworn to tell the truth, correct?"

"Yes."

"And you know that if you tell a lie you can be charged with a crime called perjury."

"Yeah, but what else can they do to me? I'm facing the death penalty already. That's at least what my lawyer told me."

"So you are a confessed killer?"

"I ain't confessed to nothing. I'm accused. I got the right to the 'sumption of innocence right??? Ain't that right Mr. Lawyerman? Ain't I entitled?"

Yao is just not as fast on his feet as he should be. She just provided so many openings, but Yao just isn't experienced enough to do that. Instead of comparing her presumption of innocence to Billy's, he says imperiously

"I'm asking the questions here, not you."

I glance at the women on the jury and all I see are uniform frowns. Ok Yao, keep it going baby keep it going.

"So you are a killer, correct?"

"My attorney has informed me that I have the right to assert my Fifth Amendment right against self-insemination and I assert that right now!!!"

"Your honor I believe that if this witness is asserting her right not to incriminate herself, that all her testimony must be struck." Yao says this with a smile and upturned face.

"Counsel you are wrong on the facts and wrong on the law. Her guilt or innocence in the two murders she is charged with is not germane to her knowledge of what happened in this case. Counsel get on with it.", barks Judge P.. Yao is clearly nonplussed he shuffles his papers and takes several awkward pauses and then abruptly sits down. Wow I guess he can't think on his feet real well. It's lunch time, so instead of calling my next witness I ask the judge if we could call our next witness after lunch. The Judge agrees and soon the courtroom is empty and I'm alone with my clients and the corrections officers. I tell Billy, "I think things are going well. Let's leave it at this ."

"I don't know JD. I think these people want and need to hear from my black ass and I think I'm gonna give it to them. "

"That's a very bad idea Billy; you cannot talk your way out of this. You can only make it worse. When not if, but when, Lok catches you in a lie, the jury will make you pay for it with their verdict".

"So says you, JD." I've smelt the alcohol on your breath the whole trial. I've had my boys spot you out at all the nightclubs and strip clubs all during this trial. If they convict me, I'm gonna get an appeal and you are gonna be exhibit one and I guarantee if they convict me this shit is coming back to haunt you. You are gonna lose your meal ticket (law license)".

With that he stands up, I sit back and smirk. This guy is an idiot, I fight my hardest for him and I have him on the brink of victory and he wants to snatch defeat away from the jaws of victory. Hey, it is his choice. I always say regardless of what happens, I go home and in this time I hope it's truly to my home and not to that damn empty condo. I get up and I head out of the courthouse towards the Inner Harbor not the BLOCK but towards Five Guys Burgers and Fries. They have the best, the tastiest burgers and fries that are so fresh. It's like they just picked the potatoes and slaughtered the cows. It's my shit. I sit down and have a double bacon cheeseburger with onions, mustard, and ketchup and Cajun fries. Man, I sit back and reload. As I sit there, I see a couple of women walk by and smile and one even waves, but for the first time since I was thirteen I was able to acknowledge the attention and continue on with my day. When I was younger, I was overweight and didn't get the attention that other guys got from women, so when I got older and started getting attention I didn't know how to handle it. Nowadays, I realize that the attention isn't because they are in love with me or because I'm just so sexy. It's because I wear a suit to work while their boyfriends are laborers. They look at me as just an upgrade over their current situation and do not give a damn about me as a person. I actually paid more attention to my food and my Blackberry as I surfed the web for the day's news. And low and behold, I see Obama is committing more troops to Afghanistan. Bro, I support you, but bring those troops and that money home to our families. I look at my gold Skagen watch (my ex-wife gave it to me for Christmas one year. I see I have fifteen minutes before Billy throws his life away, so I wrap up my meal. I gather my courage and punch my ex-wife's phone number into my cell. This time there is no male voice, but just her voicemail and I hear her cheerful voice telling people to leave their name and number after the beep. I don't do exactly what she asks (I never did that was a big part of our problems). I say, "Honey, this is Jasper. I know it's been a while, but I think I've finally come to my senses. If you would give me the chance, I'd like to be part of yours and little Jasper's lives again. I know a phone call won't do it. Promises won't do it either. But soon as I finish this murder trial, I will hop in my car and drive to see y'all. I love y'all. Have a good day, bye". I hang up as I have been walking to the courthouse the whole time.. I have five minutes left and I stop in the bathroom to check my look. I notice that for the first time in a long time I'm clean after lunch. I start wondering do I want people to know I'm back on my game. I smile a devilish grin and take a pack of ketchup out of my trial bag and I tear it open and smudge a little on my tie so it's not overwhelming, but noticeable. I stand back and look at my handiwork. They will never see me coming. I walk back to the courtroom. I can see Head and Yao arguing. They abruptly shut up when they notice me in the courtroom. I smile inwardly, knowing that my good trial work has got them pissed off. Maybe they thought this would be a cake walk with a whore chasing drunken lawyer on the other side. Now, they have bitten off more than they can chew. That shit is causing them to gag. The judge comes in and everybody rises. Billy comes in with the deputies and the judge addresses me.

"Ok, Mr. Davis, is the defendant going to testify?"

"I would invite the court to inquire."

"Mr. Johnson please stand. You remember when early today I asked you about your right to testify."

"Yes, sir your honor."

"Have you made a decision as to what you want to do?"

"Yes sir. I want to exercise my right to testify."

"Mr. Johnson, that's fine." I don't let them see the reaction on my face, but I'm pissed as hell inside. How dare this asshole ruin my chance at a guaranteed win but fine, his check cleared! I'm paid and I will go home after this. He sure as hell won't but, I will. "Mr. Davis," the judge addresses me," Do you have any other witnesses besides the defendant?'

"No, your honor."

"Ok, so we will put him on next. We will then do our jury charge conference and summations will be tomorrow at 10 a.m. Any questions, folks?" he directs to us. We both answer no your honor. Judge P. turns to his bailiff and says bring the jury in.

"Yes sir your honor."

The bailiff brings the jury in and within 3 minutes they are seated. I look at Yao. He is perched at the edge of his chair hoping, praying that my client will testify and allow him to salvage this trial. I rise and say, "The defense calls William Johnson." There is an audible gasp from the trial lawyers in the audience because they have seen the same trial I have. They know that Billy is fucking up badly. Bill saunters to the witness stand. He stands and is fidgeting big drops of sweat are rolling down his face. As he stands and takes the oath, the sweat has gotten to the point that the underarms and chest of his shirt are visibly wet. I look at the jury and every last one of them is looking at Billy with frowns on their faces and their arms crossed (to the uninitiated that in general means that people are not receptive to hear what someone has to say).

"Please state your name and quadrant of Baltimore you live in."

"I'm William Johnson and I'm from West Baltimore"... he stutters through his teeth. He just ain't ready. Testifying in front of a jury ain't a damn street hustle. The majesty of a courtroom makes Billy appear small and petty regardless of his muscle, his strength, and slick mouth. I peer at the jury; they are looking down right evil. I tell the judge.

"Your honor, my client looks a little bit parched. Could I bring him a cup of water? "Judge P. waves his hand looking mildly annoyed. I walk up to the stand with a cup and the pitcher from my trial table. I put my hand on the mic and say," Billy, can you tell if people are ready to listen to your gift of gab?" He looks at me defiantly. He gives an almost imperceptible nod of his head. While I pour his cup, I say," Look at the jury not the media in the audience. Look at the jury, dammit." I hiss. He looks over and he sees the same thing as I do. He literally shrinks in the witness stand chair. Billy resembles a frightened 6 year old instead of a thug. I tell him, "Don't do this." With a look of fear, he shakes his head yes. I return to the table and state to the judge "My client has decided not to testify." Judge P. roars

"Take the jury out."

The deputies hop to and the jury is out in record time.

"What the hell are you trying to pull Mr. Davis?"

"I'm not doing anything your honor. My client has decided that discretion is the better part of valor. It his right to not testify but he has not said anything of substance. But it has not helped his case. "

Yao interjects, "Your honor, it's not up to the defense counsel to determine what I cross examine him on. He has been sworn and has made statements on the record.

"That's true, your honor." I respond. But I have posed no questions to him beyond his name and the quadrant of his residence and his name. Cross is always limited to the subjects of direct. I would ask the court to limit the cross exam to those subjects." The judge raises his hands and says,

"Counsel, once he is sworn and takes the stand he is subject to cross exam. I can't control your direct exam, but my ruling is that he is now subject to cross examination."

148

"Well your honor I have no questions for him and intend to state that in front of the jury."

"Ok deputy bring the jury back in." We return to our tables. I look at the media in the peanut gallery. They look like they are in a feeding frenzy. This is the wackiest trial I have ever been in. I'm gonna continue to ride this sucker out. The jury comes in and is seated.

"Mr. Davis, do you have any further questions for this witness?"

"Your honor, just to keep the record clear, I don't have any questions for this witness either now or before the break. I will note for the record that I have not asked him one word beyond his name and the quadrant of Baltimore he resides in."

I sit down and Judge P. wears a dour frown. He turns to Yao and says,

"Mr. Yao, you may proceed."

Yao almost runs to the podium he asks Billy " You have a felony record right?" I hop up and object. The judge looks incredulous.

"Basis counsel?"

Beyond the scope of direct (to the uninitiated a cross exam is limited to questions and area that were covered by direct ... now a judge has the ability to give some latitude but I'm hoping Judge P. is so disgusted by this trial that he just wants it over and out of his courtroom). My wish is granted.

Judge P. crosses his arms, frowns and barks, "Objection sustain!"

Yao looks flabbergasted," But, but your honor…" he whines.

"Objection sustained. Move on Counsel."(The judge is not just worried about protecting my client's right he's more worried about being overturned on appeal.) Yao then says, "So you killed Linwood, right?"

"Objection!!!", I quip.

"Sustained", says Judge P. Yao looks flummoxed. His face is redder than a fire hydrant. He huffs and puffs and finally lets out a little strangled,

"No further questions."

Whoosh! All the air rushes out of me. Billy returns to the trial table his dark skinned face somehow looks ashen. He is quivering and quaking. Even after he sits, down his legs are quivering involuntarily as he sits down.

"Thank you JD. You saved me. I'm sorry I didn't listen to you."

I don't say anything to him I just look straight forward. Judge P. looks at me and states,

"Do you have any further witnesses, Mr. Davis?" I rise and state with full conviction,

"No more witnesses your honor." The defense rests.

Judge P. turns to the jury "Ladies and gentlemen you have heard all of the evidence in this case. It is now time for the attorneys to join me in preparing the instructions on the law that you will hear. Tomorrow, this case will be in your hands and you will begin deliberations. Please be here at 9:30. Deliberations will start at 10:00 a.m. sharp please don't be late. You are dismissed." As the jury leaves, so does the media and the other members of the peanut gallery file out as well. Charge conferences aren't sexy. In fact I don't like them myself. The only issue I want is falsus in uno. These jury instructions tell a jury that if they find that they believe that a witness testified falsely as to any issue that the jury can ignore everything else they say. I listen as the judge drones on and as Yao asks for every presumption that he can think of under the sun to help him. I snap to attention when my litigator's ear hears him ask for a flight instruction. This instruction tells the jury that by fleeing the scene of the crime the defendant exhibited a consciousness of guilt that can be considered evidence of guilt of the crime he is charged with.

"Your honor, there is absolutely no proof of flight. This was not a scene that the police responded to quickly. Not one witness said my client ran away. There is no proof that he fled the scene. Common sense dictates that anyone will leave a scene at some time. No one presumed he left his apartment or home or place of business to avoid arrest. He is alleged to simply continue traveling to his intended destination."

Judge P. says" Hum, you are right counsel. Request is denied. There simply isn't enough proof of flight. After his twentieth request, the judge says, "Counsel, do you have anything else? It seems you want me to give them every page of the handbook of model jury instructions."

"No your honor. I'm just relying on the law to carry the day." Yao responds with a simper. Yao sits down.

Judge P. says to me, "Do you have anything, Mr. Davis?"

"Yes, your honor. Just one falsus in uno..."

Yao jumps up. "Your honor that doesn't apply in this case. No witness was impeached here."

Judge P. retorts, "I don't know about you Mr. Yao, but I think I saw your whole case impeached. Request granted. Mr. Davis, anything else?"

"I just have to renew my motion for a directed verdict in this case. I don't believe a reasonable jury could, even construing the facts most favorably to the prosecution, find the defendant guilty of the charges against him."

"Motion denied. I'll see you gentleman in the morning. That's all." The corrections officer lead a still shell-shocked Billy out of the courtroom with his head hung low. I close up my bag and as I walk out, I feel really lonely. I think would it be so bad to take a left and head to Norma Jeans for just one shot of Jack and a few lap dances? I bet Shayla would be glad to see me if I walked over to her bar. I feel my body turn left towards the Block. Like a man possessed by demons, I violently fight my body and make it come to a stop. It takes all of my strength to turn around and force my body to stop as I look down at my shoes. It's my black Stacy Adams trial boots. I look at the dirt and wear and tear on them. I see a crack forming on the top of the left boot. I say to myself my life is just like that boot. I can take it to a shoe repair shop and I can save it. Or, I can continue the way I'm going. Go to strip clubs, drink, and chase whores and I'll be just as useless as this boot will be when it's busted. It's time for me to go home. I exhale deeply and I head up towards my condo. I may be alone, but its time I get to know myself. Besides, I have to get ready for my closing. It's not the time to slip slide when a man's life is in your hands. Even when you know the dirty mutherfucker did it. In fact when you know he did it, it's definitely time to work harder. My job is to try and free the guilty in spite of their actions. I walk into my apartment. I feel a stress headache coming on. I feel chills and my body has the shakes. It seems I have the DT's from withdrawal, since I have given up on cheap sex and booze. I actually start having the dry heaves. I sit down heavily at the kitchen table, spit some acid on the floor. I go to my bathroom and take my prescription Nexium out of the bathroom cabinet and pop two down my throat. I can either let my body cause me to give up or I can handle my business. I think I'm gonna handle my business. I'm not gonna let my old addictions force me to throw in the towel. I stare at my face at the bathroom mirror and I like what I see. The swelling has gone down, but I no longer look so rat like. My teeth don't seem so sharp and my nose doesn't seem elongated and furry. As I've stopped giving into my desires. I found a way to come back to myself. I'm gonna be A- ok. I'm just gonna have to fight for myself the rest of my life. I collapse onto my lazy boy, pull out the leg rest, and lay back. I reach over to my left and pull my notebook out. I commence to prepare my summation for Billy's trial. It's gonna take a doozy to save this asshole. I stay up 'til 1:30 am. I then yawn, stretch, and I put away my computer. I lay on my back in bed. As I stretch out, I notice that I'm hard as a mutherfucking rock. I have a choice. I can call somebody to come handle this for me or I can jack off. Let me see call a woman and get entangled again or I can jack off and go to sleep. I could spend more money and risk disease from a professional. I decide that if the five fingers can't get it done, it won't get it done. And surprisingly enough, they get it done. I feel sleepy and I surrender my eyes to sleep (surprise that I jacked off. Why? I never said I was gonna be a monk, just not a whore anymore ... if loving yourself is a crime I don't want to be right. Holla) and with that thought I fall asleep.

CHAPTER 19

Closing arguments

AS MY ALARM GOES off at seven, I struggle to get up and to my feet. I lurch to my feet and go the bathroom to take a piss that sounds like a river roaring thru a canyon. I guess the poisons in my body are saying bye- bye to my system. I feel relieved and relax when the urine cuts off and I stretch and a short fart comes out my butt. I scratch my belly and walk back into the main part of the apartment. I look at my suits and I resolve that after this trial I'm gonna burn all these suits and start all over. I pick the least dirty suit, which happens to be my favorite black Wal-Mart suit that was made in the Dominican Republic. The shirt I wore yesterday is still fresh. I have to replace the tie with a royal blue tie that my wife bought for me. I quickly shave my head and trim my goatee. I splash my head and face with Old Spice aftershave and rub it down with Vaseline. Man, I look good. I throw on my suit and shoes and grab my trial bag and I'm off to go to war against Yao.

This is gonna be good.

Now why Yao isn't the best trial lawyer - there is a reason why the DA's office calls him the strongest finisher in the game? Yao can bring a closing argument home to a jury not because of antics or histrionics; he can do it because he does not get himself in front of the argument. He doesn't make his personality stand out over the facts. He gives them just enough dressing for them to stand up on their own. But I'm gonna make his simple ass pay for his simple words this time. As I break into the courthouse the mob of media is milling around the lobby. The second they see me, microphones are shoved in my face.. And you know what I say? "Gather around and I will give you a statement." I notice that it's not only local media but now the national media (including Tru TV, the successors to Court TV) are there as well as national PBS , CBS , Fox and CNN. I spot the MSNBC camera, and I give a shout out to my main whigger Keith Olberman. As the media pulls together I say, "I just want to tell my wife and son that I love them and I want to come home." The media gets a strange look on their face and I stride away into the courtroom. As they try to come together and figure out what I have just done and what they have just heard. Oh shit. Now I'm sure they will dig into my marital history and that will be the story on the midday news. But maybe my ex will hear that or see it and it will bring her smile back to her face. A smile that my bad acts (bad is an understatement) took away from her.

I walk to my table and Billy is sitting there already. He looked at me. "Are you ready JD? What's gonna happen?"

"The judge is going to instruct the jury on the law. Then I'm gonna sum up. Then the state's attorney is gonna sum up and then the jury will deliberate and attempt to come back with a verdict."

"You make it sound so simple JD. This is my damn life."

"Well good. Now that you acknowledge that, next time don't put yourself in this position ever again and pray to God that you get another chance to change your life. Billy hangs his head towards his chest and his but lie detector goes off again. I guess not from lying, but from fear that in the next few hours, his life will be up to twelve people whose qualifications are they don't know Billy and they said they could be fair. That's a hell of a lot to depend on from someone else. (To the uninitiated never put yourself in this situation and your life won't be in someone else's hands).

Judge shuffles his way into the courtroom. He looks every day of his 65 years. It seems like a big weight is on his shoulders.

"Judge is everything ok?" both Yao and I approach.

"It's ok gentlemen. I was just told that the young lady you called yesterday committed suicide while in custody. She realized that the rest of her life was going to be in a cage and she couldn't handle it. She hung

154

herself with her bed sheets from the bars of her cell last night." Judge P. breathes heavily.

I have never seen a case so saddled with tragedy as this one. I can't fathom the huge loss of life that surrounds this case and wonder if man's inhumanity to man will ever end. I stand there silently and hang my head. I think about how hopeless that Laquaana felt, how alone she had to be to do that to herself. I wondered if I had done that if the US Marshals had locked me up instead of her. I had been facing the death penalty. Would I have done the same? A tear rolls down from my eye (not for Laquaana, but for myself). I realize that I've been given a second chance and I swear before God, I'm gonna make the best of it.

"Your honor, I would ask that I be allowed to tell my client this after the jury is out. He has enough to worry about without bringing this into the mix."

The judge shakes his head," Very well. Step back gentlemen. Are you ready to begin summation?"

"Yes your honor," we both chorus. I notice that the peanut gallery is packed full and there are not a small number of media figures and expert legal commentators in the courtroom. I even see Nancy Grace, but all she does is glare at me and takes a seat in the prosecution side of the courtroom. Figures... Everything else I block out. As I sit there, the judge drones on for 35 minutes on the jury instructions. I steel myself for my argument. Maryland is quirky in that the state gets to argue twice. First they bring up their direct arguments then they get to argue to rebut my arguments after I sum up, which is a pretty good advantage. I just gotta be ready and throw Yao off his game so he can't rebut because I have always seen that when I make a good argument and the prosecution fails to respond to my argument in their rebuttal, it always helps to carry the day.

So As Judge P. finishes up he then turns to Yao and says "Mr. Yao the jury is with you."

Yao is wearing a navy blue suit with a pocket kerchief and a black tie and a shockingly white shirt. Oh boy he's gonna pull out all stops to look severe and foreboding.... "Ladies and gentleman of the jury, I thank you for the three weeks you have taken out of your life to hear this evidence in this case. On behalf of the state of Maryland, I want to thank you for your time and attention on behalf of the people of the state of Maryland. I'm sure when you came into the courtroom, you didn't expect to be facing such horrible facts. A man beaten to death because another man, that man sitting over there" pointing at my client "William Johnson aka Billy Badass wanted his car, an old car at that. Is that how much a human life is worth? You heard from Officer Pregrum that car had a blue book value of $750 bucks. Wasn't Linwood White worth more than $750 dollars? Wasn't his life worth more than that? "

"In this case, you heard testimony from several witnesses, but I think you need to look closest at the testimony of Markey Fortune. Markey told you he saw the murder. He wasn't involved. He knew both parties and he watched Billy Badass stomp Linwood to death. He talked about seeing him stomp on the victim's head with Timberland boots and seeing blood spurt out of the victim's ears. Mr. Fortune heard the argument and knew that it was about the car. That Linwood White was slain by Billy Badass for a car worth $750.You have the testimony of Laquaana Richardson who told you she was Billy's girlfriend and she was with him from the minute he arrived on the scene. She saw him beat and stomp the life out of the man . She saw the blood spurt out of Linwood White's head. She knows her boyfriend and had no motive to lie. Now, she did come back in here and tried to change her story. Don't you let her. Hold her to what she said. Listen to the details of what she said. Is there any dispute, any testimony that contradicts what she said the first time I submit to you now?"

"I object," I say.

The judge interrupts and says, "Jury it's your recollection that controls. If the attorneys say something that you remember differently, your memory controls or if you are uncertain you can request a read back of testimony. Counsel please proceed."

The judge is absolutely right, your memory controls.

"You heard the testimony of the coroner as to how Linwood White died. You heard the testimony and saw the pictures of his beaten and broken body." Yao walks over to his trial table and takes up a blowup of Linwood's body lying in a bloody pool, lifeless on the ground and places it on an easel to the right front of the jury. I notice several women and a few women become uneasy as they take a look at the picture before them. Fine Yao, let them be distracted by the photo. How can they hear what you say? The photo speaks for itself. If he were a better trial lawyer he would let the photo stand on the easel for thirty seconds shut up and let it speak for itself. But here he goes continuing his argument. Hey, it helps my client, so I keep my damn mouth shut.

Yao drones on "you heard testimony from Roxanne, Linwood's girlfriend as to what she saw. How she saw her boyfriend lying, bleeding to death in her arms and how she saw his skull crushed in several places and how he breathed his last breath in her arms. How she was covered in his blood and felt numb from his pain. She saw the agony of his death first hand. In fact, there she is. Look at her. Can you not give her justice for the death of her boyfriend? How can you look in her eyes and say this killer doesn't deserve to be punished for what he did to the man she loved."

As you watch, you see tears run down Roxanne's face and she breaks out in wretched sobs. I actually busy myself with my computer. Damn, she is better than I thought.

"Ladies and gentleman, I'm asking you to give me justice. I'm asking you to come back the only verdict consistent with the credible evidence in this case, the only verdict consistent with justice...a verdict of guilty." (Dammit he stole my line. I've been using that line since I was a rookie trying misdemeanors. Ok he's trying to get under my skin. He's trying but I'm better than that. I gonna get him.)

Judge P. looks at me and says the jury is now with the defense. I sit at the table slumped down in my chair with my hands in my pockets for a count of twenty seconds. Judge P. has seen me do this before so he doesn't react. I see him grinning in the bench. He's thinking good ole JD. He's back.

"Ladies and gentleman of the jury, I want to thank you for the time and attention you have paid to this case not just on behalf of the state but on behalf of every ordinary citizen of this state whose rights are guaranteed against unfair prosecution by the jury system you have been a part of for the last three weeks. You stand hand in hand and shoulder to shoulder from the current time to the jurors of ancient Greece who started the tradition of fellow citizens hearing accusations against their fellow citizens. Now the judge has given you the law and all that is left for you to do is for you to use that law as a guide as you find the facts of what happened here. Now before you can decide what to believe, you have to determine whom to believe. You see this is not a case where the physical evidence establishes guilt. It's undisputed that my client touched the steering wheel of Mr. White's car so it is expected that has fingerprints would be there. You don't have bloody boots that the prosecution said my client wore. You don't have any bloody clothing that it is alleged my client wore and you don't have a video or pictures of the murders even though there is a Baltimore police camera in the area."

Yao jumps up and yells "Objection!"

Judge P. growls "I don't remember any testimony of cameras being in this area."

"Judge, if I could refer to the prosecution's own evidence. I'm referring to the state's 35 mm evidence, the photo of the victim's body." I take the photo that shows Linwood's body and I point into the upper right corner, lo and behold, there is a Baltimore police department camera box that is clear and apparent and with a blue light on top.

Yao drops to his chair like he was hit with a Mike Tyson punch to his midsection.

Judge P. raises his eyebrows and says, "Please proceed." The smile on his face is clearly perceptible.

I hear more than see Sadie titter. My clerk fan is in my corner again. I point to the blowup that Yao has made and it is clearly seen. You can even see the warning on the box that the area is being recorded. I restrain myself from laughing. How did all those prosecutors and homicide detectives miss that in front of their face?

"Where is the recording from that camera? Why wasn't it produced for you? Why did they have to rely on a cast of characters? Now let's take the police officers that responded to the murder out of the case because they didn't see anything, they didn't witness anything or see anything; they just relied on the faulty statements of people who had a lot to gain. First, let's look at Markey Fortune. Markey told you he regularly works his cases off with the police by testifying against other people so how can you trust what he says. He told you that he just stood there and watched another person murdered and did nothing. That's a Good Samaritan? Huh? What type of monster watches a murder and does nothing to help the victim, doesn't call the police, doesn't try to help him? Just watches and comes forward only when it would help him. How can you rely on him?"

The next witness they brought in was Elvira. "Now you heard her tell you that she testifies for the police regularly. So regularly, it's her regular paycheck, it's her weekly job and she got paid on her job to testify in this case. She is a drug addict and neither she nor Mr. Fortune told you where they were hiding when they witnessed the incident. Wouldn't you want to know that? Why didn't the prosecutor ask that? You may ask 'why didn't I ask them that?' but do you remember in voir dire that you understood that the burden lays on the prosecutor's table and you all said you could understand that and wouldn't hold my client to the burden of proving anything. So it would fall to them to ask, not me. You heard testimony from Roxanne about seeing Linwood lying dying and beaten on the ground but did she ever tell you my client did those actions? No. The prosecutor asked you to look in her eyes and give her justice. That's fine. But give her the justice of convicting someone in which there has been proof beyond a reasonable doubt. Not just asking for retribution not just blaming anyone but blame the person who it's been proven did this. Justice isn't a faceless raving monster. It blinks and only when the scales are tipped beyond a reasonable doubt, do you convict. Justice demands that you look into Roxanne's eyes and give her justice not retribution. Let's look lastly at the testimony of Laquaana Richardson. She told you when she returned in a jump suit, she was told by a federal officer to testify to what she did by a federal officer who was her lover and my client's rival, a federal agent who was hiding money and planning to flee the country, a federal agent who she killed. The state's attorney asks you to trust and believe that testimony. They actually had the gall to tell you that the testimony of Ms. Richardson was uncontroverted, uncontroverted. She contradicted it herself when I called her. She told you she was told to testify that way by a crooked DEA agent. How can you rely on that ladies and gentlemen? If one officer of the law would tell witnesses to lie does it seem so far-fetched that that same officer or other officers would tell other witnesses to lie? This is a case where you have smoking gun that points at the prosecution. They bring you a crop of corrupt witnesses and they tell you to believe these people. Ask yourselves would you rely on the word of Markey Fortune or Elvira or Laquaana Richardson to do anything? Would you let them tell you where to eat lunch? Not even consider letting them tell you who to marry or what house to buy. Would you trust their words in the most important of your affairs? Would you trust their words in any of your affairs? I that answer is no, can you trust their words here in the most important of human affairs, a murder trial? Ask yourselves 'where is the video of the murder? Where are the witnesses out there who don't frequently testify for the police" Where is the everyday citizen who saw this and comes forward as a Good Samaritan? Where is that? Don't reward the state for bringing a case so full of fraud and plain greedy gain. Their whole premise doesn't make sense. They told you the motive for this case is that my client wanted the car but the car never leaves the scene. It's there when Linwood is there with the keys in it. They want to bring you to the outrage of a man murdered for a car worth $750.00 bucks. Well bring your outrage and show the state that you won't tolerate black men being sent to jail on the words of proven felons and liars and rogue agents.

Now the way this game is played, I have to sit down now and the prosecution gets to speak again. I don't ask you to ignore the state just listen to them critically. Don't just listen with a sympathetic ear. Be critical. When he makes an argument ask yourself what would Mr. Davis say about that? What's wrong with what he just said? I ask you to bring back the only verdict consistent with justice; the only one consistent with the spirit of justice, honesty, and the American way, which is a verdict of not guilty. As I pace to my desk, I hear a smattering of applause from the peanut gallery. Judge P. quickly restores order with a tap of his gavel. "Mr. Yao does the state have a rebuttal argument?"

"Of course they do, and I know it by heart. It's that if this were a big conspiracy case, then why would we all be out to get William Johnson, a conspiracy that covers state and federal officers and physical evidence and private citizens. If it isn't then what we have is a defendant that is guilty of murder of an innocent man. Look in your heart and souls and bring back the only verdict that can exist in this case (uh oh never tell the jury you don't have a choice because they will come back and show you that they have a choice and it's the exact opposite one you told them they had to bring back). I see several jurors frown and fold their arms as Yao says that, but he is so busy talking he doesn't seem to be paying attention to what the jury is saying with their body language.

Not good, homeboy, not good. As he ends and returns to his seat, the judge tells the jury:

"Your first duty is to elect a foreman who will speak for the jury and present and sign the verdict sheet. The sheet speaks for itself. I will just tell you now. "Go forth and do justice" (and in my mind I think "or a reasonable facsimile.") The jury walks into the jury room and the door closes with a cool finality.

Billy looks at me." Now what do we do?"

"We wait Billy. We just wait." With that, the corrections officers shackle him and bring him back to the pens downstairs. I wait at the trial table. The judge walks out, the media files out to file their reports and Yao goes upstairs to his office. As I sit there, I put my feet up on the trial table, hands behind my head and lean back. Now it is a waiting game and my role is done. As usual, at this point, all of my adrenalin drains out of me and I feel dog-tired almost immediately. Man that was the craziest trial I have ever seen. I fall into a power nap and 35 minutes later a deputy taps my shoulder and I look around and see everyone is in the courtroom but the jury and they are looking at me. Shit. This can't be happening. Judge P. smirks and says, "We will send the jury to lunch now since it is noon. You are all excused until two. Enjoy your lunch. Mr. Davis, enjoy your nap. You've earned it." With that, I know that I have worked my way back into the judge's good graces again. I'm reborn hard. I'm a man again. I walk to my condo set my alarm clock and set my clock for 90 minutes from now and knock the fuck out. I dream of my ex coming home to her and seeing my son and playing catch with him. I dream of being home in front of the fireplace with them. I feel tears running down my face and when I reawake at 1:30 my face and pillow are wet with tears. I get up warily and hold my face in my hands and wipe the tears away. I've got to find a way to get my family back. I need them and I know they need me and who the hell was that that answered my phone. There better not be another man in that house trying to raise my son. Jesus, I gave up so much for alcohol and sex addiction. Why could I throw so much away? I get dressed and walk back to the courthouse. At two promptly, the judge comes back in and says, "The jury is resuming deliberations and we are to remain at ease." While I sit there, I contemplate writing a novel about the last three weeks of my life but who would believe me. I fought a sex addiction, gave up alcohol, and became a responsible adult again all while trying a violent first-degree murder case. Man, this world is a trip. As I wait, I start thinking about the office and all the work I have sitting there waiting me. I also am thinking what it will take for me to go home to my woman and son.

Meanwhile I sit there at my desk. Sadie comes over to me. "Jasper, have you gotten yourself together?"

"Yes ma'am I have."

"I'm so glad. I was so afraid for you when it seemed like you were going off the deep end. Jasper, these women out here will ruin you just for sport. Focus on family and work and let God take care of the rest," she says as she pats my shoulder.

I say "thank you ma'am." My heart is genuinely warmed by her actions. It lets me know that she does care about me. That's nice to know. I spend so much of my time alone, I feel like that the only people I have been around are hookers and criminals and that can't be healthy.

As the minutes turn to hours, Judge P. returns and the case is adjourned for tomorrow for further deliberations. As I walk out of the courtroom, who do I see outside waiting for me, but Carmen? I don't know how to react. I don't need to panic and I don't. But dammit, she will not hit me again. I'm not down for that shit.

Carmen walks up and says, "I'm sorry Jasper. I should have never hit you. If you want to have me arrested, I will admit it and take my medicine."

"Carmen, no real man reports a woman for hitting him, especially when I deserved it."

Carmen's eyes water. "Why can't we give this another chance?"

"Because Carmen, I'm just getting to know myself again and I can't be with someone else till I know who I am again and I think right now I have some unfinished business with my ex and until that is resolved, it wouldn't be fair to drag other people into my mess. Life is difficult enough without dragging other people in my mess. I'm sorry Carmen but our timing isn't right."

Carmen reaches and gives me a big hug she feels soft through her white sweater and skirt and my nether regions start to react. I slowly push her away. I'm not going to be a slave to my loins anymore. I've got a brain and I'm gonna use it.

"Thank you Carmen, but I gotta go. I'll see you around." She walks away as I see a small tear run out of the corner of her left eye. Not so long ago I would have felt responsible for her pain and would have done everything to stop her pain. But I'm not responsible and we are responsible only to the people for whom we accept responsibility. I had a responsibility to my ex to stop her tears, but I never did. I was the one that caused her tears. As I breathe a heavy sigh, I remember that when I was married, I cared more for other people's feelings than I did for my own wife's. It is time for me to let go and accept responsibility only for those I love not those I lust. I head towards my apartment and for the first time in three weeks I turn on my TV. At the top of the 5:30 news there I am telling my ex I love her. That's all right. I didn't think they would carry it. But as I listen to the audio, they list this among the many strange behaviors that have been seen from attorney Jasper Davis in the last three weeks of this trial. The anchor asks the on scene reporter, "the attorney doesn't seem to be losing it does he?"

"To the contrary, he gave an extraordinary closing and seemed to get better and stronger as the trial wore on. I guess the trial has kept him away from his family so long that he had to let them know he still loves them." That makes me laugh and smile. I remember that there is a football game and I want to see it. As a reflex action, I walk towards the refrigerator and grab a beer (I didn't throw them out when I tossed out the Jack. Beer has never been my addiction). I flip the channel and tune it to the Raven's game. My man Ray Lewis handles his business. As I sit there, I feel the cold goodness of that Bud Lite pour down my throat before I know it I have consumed a six-pack and I'm looking around for more beer. The game is in the fourth quarter with 5 minutes left to go, but I want another beer so bad that I walk out to the corner liquor store with my team driving and down by four. But it's on my mind and I rationalize that if I wait I will not be able to get the beer later. So I walk into the store and wait in line behind two drunks whose clothes have seen better days and I wait my turn. I get to the counter and I buy a case of Bud Lite. As I walk back to my building, I all of a sudden feel a cold peace of metal stick in the back of my neck. I hear a rough male voice say, "Run that son!"

"Run that? What the hell is he talking 'bout?"

He then says, "You already know what it is."

I turn around because I'm so confused by his Ebonics I don't want to do the wrong thing and get shot and as I turn around, but who do I see in a dirty grey hoodie sweat shirt but Markey Fortune.

"Markey, what are you doing?"

"Oh shit, JD. Yo. I'm sorry he says as he lowers the gun. What the fuck you doing out this late by yourself, JD? You know its robbing time. Man, you a bold mutherfucka coming out for beer at this late hour. I would have waited my black ass until the next morning to come out. Damn, JD I thought you knew. Yo can I have a beer bro?"

I open the case and hand Markey two beers and I walk the last ten feet into my building and the door shuts behind me. My heart finally drops down from my throat back to the proper place. I look at the case of beer and realize I just risked my fucking life for another beer. Damn, I can't even drink this shit casually watching football. I can't control myself. I could have died tonight on the streets of Baltimore over beer. I promptly walk over to the trash bin and toss the case in. I walk up to my apartment. Close the door. Turn off the lights and TV and spend the rest of the night staring at the ceiling until I fall asleep and just before I go unconscious, I feel a single tear run out of my left eye down my cheek to the pillow and I know all that I have and could regain could have been lost because of my love of alcohol tonight. My son would have been fatherless and who would provide for him and my wife, I mean ex-wife. There isn't anything such as a little sober or a little saved. It's either all or nothing. So it's time for me to be all in.

CHAPTER 20

Waiting game

I WAKE UP THE next morning hung over but sober in spirit. I know what I am and what life I have chosen. I'm not mad at the headache. It feels good because I know it's the last time that I will ever be hung over from alcohol. The pain is self-affirming. In fact it affirms the fact that I have abstained for quite a while. It's been a long time since I have had a hangover. You see your body has to clear itself from alcohol for a hangover to take effect. I have probably been continuously intoxicated for the last few years so I haven't dried out enough to have a hangover.

Today is a waiting game. You never know how quick a jury will come back. It could come back in five minutes or it could be days or they could comeback hung. Back when I was a new attorney, this time was nerve wracking for me. I would frustrate myself trying to think what the jury has in their heads. What are they thinking? What are they focusing on? What could I have done better? What have I forgotten? But as I grew in experience and time, I knew that the only thing I could do is wait. Frustrating myself wouldn't make my life any easier or better and it wouldn't make the jury do what they were gonna do any faster. It was just going to give me stress and headaches. So I grab my iPod and slide it into my briefcase. I'm dressed in one of my old suits. I gotta go to Walmart and replace it. Nonetheless, I put on a tan suit with a blue shirt and I grab a red tie and I hit the door. As I walk out, I see the two Asian girls who went from being my fuck buddies to cold strangers. They both look at me with looks of daggers, knives, and any other sharp object you can think of. A few days ago, that would have meant something to me but now it doesn't. Their feelings aren't my concern. I owe them nothing and want nothing to do with them. I owe only my family and myself. Random women who gave me their bodies got mine in return and they aren't entitled to my emotions, feelings, and caring or money. Since I won't be dealing with them anymore, it's good to know that I can be free of them forever and be available to my family who deserve everything I have. I walk out the door confident and ready to face whatever the world has to offer me. Once again, I go on my route to the courthouse. I just keep wondering if my wife would want to have anything to do with me. I mean, doesn't forgiveness have to have its limits? For the last five years I have been a whoremonger, a cheater, and an alcoholic. Some may even call me a letch, a man who put his body's desires ahead of everything, including my son who I haven't seen in five years. I know I told you before my trial started that I saw him once a week, but hell you had to notice I've been on trial for three weeks and you ain't heard one damn word of me heading to Lake Norman and visiting him right? I haven't seen my son in five years. I haven't held him or talked to him. I told his mom when I left that if she wouldn't have me then I was leaving them both. Shocking isn't it? I'm a bigger scumbag than you ever knew, right? As I'm walking, I feel tears streaming down my face. I take hard breaths and realize for the first time in a long time I'm crying not for myself but for my son and ex. They never deserved the shitty way I treated them. I know I wasn't myself, but how do I show them I'm different? How do I assure myself that I am different? I just don't know. I'm so tired of being a criminal defense attorney (emphasis on criminal). I may have saved my career by not drinking and not whoring, but the bigger question is how can I save my life how can I be the man I'm supposed to be instead of the child who was a slave to his desires? I think I gotta go to church. I'm torn because I'm due in court in 15 minutes. Who can I talk to? Point blank I'm not a Christian. I'm spiritual but not in the God fearing fire and brimstone sense. I pick up my Blackberry and call Judge P.'s chambers. The court clerk picks up and says, "Hello".

"Yes, Ms. Sadie this is JD. I was hoping to talk to Judge P.?"

"An exparte communication?"

I tell her I just had a family emergency and I need the judge to let the jury go back into deliberations without me being present.

Ms. Sadie says," Hold on. Let me tell the Judge." I hear the Judge's gruff voice in the background saying,

"What? What's going on? Let me talk to him. Judge P. gets on the phone and says, "JD. What the hell is going on? "

"Judge I just need an hour. I know you noticed the change I've made in my career. I just need to make a change in my life overall. I have the utmost respect for you and your court. I just need to do something to make sure I can be the man I need to be for my family." Judge P.'s hard edge voice softens for the first time I have heard in ten years.

"Son, take your time and get your family life together. I'm proud of the change I have seen in you in this trial and I'll help do anything to keep you back on the straight and narrow. Go on son, handle your business. I'll see you by 11:00 am." With that he hangs up the phone. I hail a cab and I take it to Fort McHenry. I walk the grounds of where Francis Scott Key wrote the national anthem. I can't get focused on how to preserve my life. I spend a good hour walking around and glancing at the harbor. It just doesn't help. I just walk down the hill back to the street and my heart is just as heavy as it was when go there. As I wait for a train to arrive. A little old man that is clearly a street guy walks up to me. His breath is fetid but he asks, "Can you hook a brotha up? Can I have a few bucks?" Usually I ignore the street guys. The last time I gave a street guy a buck, it was three years ago. I gave a guy 5 dollars to watch my car while I went around the corner to the Block. When I came back two hours later, that fucker had broken the passenger window of my car and stole my damn laptop. Fucker! But for this one time, I say fuck it. I reach in my pocket and take two loose dollars and a quarter out of my pocket and hand it to him. He takes it in his grimy hands and says,

"You know the secret to a happy life is to love those who love you. And that love is shown through your actions." I could have been knocked over by a feather. This guy wasn't a Ph.D. (at least I don't think he was. In this economy anything is possible). This guy summed up what I've been feeling more than a little while. I've said it to myself, but I just needed to hear it from some other person. My wife will know I love her because of my total commitment to her. As I get in a yellow cab, I start plotting my way back into my family's life. As the cab arrives at the courthouse, I see it's only ten thirty. I go into Courtroom 5-2 to check in; I wave at Ms. Sadie. She smiles and acknowledges me. The courtroom is deserted. There is nothing to see until the jury comes. I set myself up at the defense table. I kick my feet up on the table and lean back and think about where my life is going. Thirty minutes into my nap, I'm awakened by a sharp rapping from the jury room door. Aww shit, that can only mean one thing: a verdict. I put my feet down and my heart rate picks up. I know I go home regardless but a jury verdict isn't just a judgment on your client's guilt. It's a judgment on your ability as a trial lawyer. It's judgment on Jasper Davis, Esq. Attorney At Law. Am I a big swinging dick or a little peewee? Maybe I need to stop thinking of myself as a sex organ. I smile and give myself a little private chuckle. Hey! I'll be ok. Either way I go home. And the truth is I hope I go home not just to my fucked up little condo, but to Lake Norman to my family. As I wait for the jury to come in the courtroom, the peanut gallery is filling in. I finger my Blackberry. Maybe I should call my wife. Back in the day when we were still together I used to call her when the jury came in and I would lay the phone somewhere the court wouldn't notice it, so she could hear the jury's verdict at the same time I would. She shared my highs and lows and was right there with me as my career progressed. Why did my dick take her away from me? I start to call her and I see the judge walk in. So I complete the dial and I leave the phone sitting to my left perched on top of my trial bag. I don't know if it's an open line or voice mail but I want her to share this with me, as the deputy shouts "All rise." The courtroom has three times the number of deputies it had before. The court wants to make sure that there isn't a dust up if he's convicted or acquitted. They want to know that if he's acquitted or convicted that people in the courtroom don't a fool or that Billy doesn't act a fool. Man you wouldn't believe what I have seen. I've seen a victim's family attack an acquitted defendant and whoop him like a runaway slave. I've seen a convicted murderer fight 5 deputies hand to hand breaking noses, faces, and kneecaps. There is no more intense outpouring of emotion known to human kind than the reading of a verdict of a murder case. As time grows closer and the court fills, my neck constricts. I just keep telling myself regardless, I go home. No matter what they say or convict Billy of, I go home. I'm repeating this so much it's like a mantra. Man, I don't know what else I can do. I'm having trouble breathing when in walks the corrections officers with Billy. His knees are shaking so bad that it is audible when he is still twenty feet away from me. He smells even worse than he looks. God, the next time I try a first degree murder, I will wear a gasmask. God, this man did not pay me enough money to have to smell his bowels as well as defend him. I tell Billy that they have a verdict and to control his emotion regardless of what happens because the judge will; be watching him. He has to understand that in Maryland a life sentence make you eligible for parole in fifteen years and he could sentence you to less than that.(I neglect to tell him that no one has ever gotten parole off of a murder life sentence in Maryland, but hey that's just semantics). The judge strides in and the courtroom is so tense that you could cut the stress with a switchblade. As the deputy yells, "All rise!"

Every one hops up. Billy is so weak he can barely stand he looks like Stepin Fetchit in one of those old movies. It's hard to believe that this is the same cockstrong arrogant asshole that used to come to my office all the time and brag about how he was crossing them over and making more money that Mobil Oil. Like I said, there is a way that a courtroom can break you down. If you don't believe me look at video of any of those so called titans of industry who ended up in court like Madoff. They don't look like the kings of anything when they are chained up and before the Judge. The judge tells the bailiff to bring the jury into the courtroom. And when they walk in, I have never seen such a foreboding group of people in my life. They refuse to look at anyone. I look at Yao and he looks at me. Neither one of us can figure out a damn thing. They sit down and just then they all turn their fire glances on at Billy. Uh oh, the jig is up they hate him and they are gonna take their anger out on him and convict him. I feel like I'm gonna shrink in to my chair. I want to be anywhere else but here. I feel like a failure. I look at my Blackberry with the open line and I guess the first thing my wife will hear from me is me failing at trial. Judge P. directs the jury hand the verdict to the bailiff. The bailiff walks over to the jury foreman, my homie with the ankh ring. He takes it and walks the folded paper to Judge P. The judge opens it with a snap and looks at the verdict. His eyes rise up to a point of surprise. I sit up quickly. What's going on I think? The judge hands the verdict to Ms. Sadie and directs her to take the verdict. The Judge directs the defendant to rise and like always I rise with my client. The time of the verdict is not time to abandon your client no matter how badly you want to do that. Ms. Sadie tells the jury to rise. They rise and she directs her question to the jury foreman.

"How do you say on the charge that William Johnson did murder Linwood White in the first degree by beating him with hands and feet causing him to die?"

"Not guilty" the jury foreman spat out like it tasted like rotted food. Yao looks deflated.

"How does the jury say on count two of the indictment that William Johnson committed second degree murder by beating Linwood White to death with hands and feet?

"Not guilty" says the jury foreman who hung his head and several women on the jury seem to be crying. I fall back towards my chair, but before I can hit the chair; Billy turns and grabs me before my butt hits the chair.

He says" You did it JD! You saved my life. I owe you everything I owe you. He says between big tears. Then he lets go. All I can hear is the judge banging his gavel yelling for order. I see the deputies close in on Linwood's family who are trying to climb over the bar and get at Billy. Whether they know it or not they are lucky that the deputies stop them. Billy would have stomped all of them to death as well. As the jury files out Yao stands up and says loudly"

"Your honor the defendant won't be released because there is a detainer from Washington ,DC where he has a pending murder trial."

I smirk. I know Yao did that to tell the jury not so subtly that they have just freed a murderer. Judge P. calls both me and Yao to the bench and says directly to us both "Gentlemen you tried an excellent trial and I'm glad to know such excellent attorneys appear before me each and every day. Good luck gentlemen. You are free to go to the jury room to talk to the jury if you like. I'm kind of hesitant, but Judge P. says, "I would take it as a personal favor if you do that." The jury always has questions for you all that I can never answer. After seeing the looks on their faces, it's the last place I want to be. I owe Judge P. and regardless of what they say I go home. As I reach for my bag, at my trial table, I see the Blackberry is still on with an open line. I pick up the phone and say, "Hello," and I hear the voice of an angel.

"Good work JD! You haven't lost your touch. I saw you on Court TV or I guess Tru TV, you're still a good trial lawyer."

"I'm trying to be a better person not just a trial lawyer. I've stopped drinking and whoring and now I just want to be human again."

"Well I'm sure you can be. There are now gonna be a lot of trial opportunities there for you."

"The only opportunity I want is to see you and my son." I hear silence on the phone for the next twenty seconds.

"You can't just walk in and out of your son's life. Talk to me when you have time to concentrate on that issue alone." And then I hear the phone click. Even in a courtroom full of defendants, cops, prosecutors, and media, I am all alone. As I proceed to the jury room, Yao walks over and shakes my hand and say Good job JD. I thought I had you."

I reply," Yao you never had me. You almost had Billy, but you never had me." I then push through the jury room and the jury is staring daggers at me as I walk in the room. All at once they start yelling.

"You're a prick JD. You're an asshole how could you defend a scum bag like that?"

The foreman said, "We think he did it but you did such a good job we couldn't be sure beyond a reasonable doubt".

I realize this isn't a place where I want to be so I say, "Ladies and gentleman, I will say this and I will be gone .Every hates defense attorneys until they or someone in their family needs one. Then we're heroes. Have a good day. And it was nice meeting you." The room is so quiet a pin drop could be heard. With that I slip out the door, grab my trial bag, and head out the door. My cell phone rings and it's Jeff.

"Hey, Billy you must have won because our phone is ringing off the hook with interview opportunities. Defendants from up and down the East Coast want to retain our firm and they're talking big cash retainers."

"You know I'm gonna come in tomorrow and talk to you about that."

"Ok, ok. Go home, rest; go get your freak on. How about the Hustler Club? My treat. All that top shelf booty wiggling at you. "

"No Hustler Club. I just want to go home. I have some things I need to work out and I need to get some real deep sleep."

As I walk to my condo I'm plotting the next step, the next stage of my life. As I walk in my building, I decide that it's time for me to shake my life up and turn a new leaf. I walk to my apartment. I look at my watch it's 2:00 in the afternoon. I get another call from Jeff.

"Hey Billy's people want to retain you for his DC trial and he wants you to come over to East Eager Street and talk to him ASAP."

"I'll go tomorrow morning before I come in to the office."

"Great, JD the money is rolling in. You sure you don't want to go out and see some fat asses shaking; you've earned it. Jeff, I've earned a lot but that's not something I want or earned."

"Did I reach the right phone is this JD? Hello, who is this? Is this the Archbishop or is this JD?? Hello??" I laugh and punch the hang up button. I sit down in my easy chair and I start plotting the next stage of my life. I call the Salvation Army and I ask them to come and pick up my furniture tomorrow. I call a realtor and ask them to list my apartment for sale immediately. They are flabbergasted, since I'm in one of the most desired buildings in B'more. I walk over to my bed and I lay down with my hands behind my head. I stay like that until I fall asleep. I wake up and it's 8:00 pm. I wonder, am I really ready to change my life now? Am I ready to be a husband and father again? I do something I haven't done in 7 years. I pick up the phone and I call my dad. Yes. JD "Mr. Jack" Daniels wasn't born of a she wolf and a horny toad; I have a family. I had lost my mom a few years back. I don't like to talk about that, but she was the glue that held my family together, and without her, we really fell apart and away from each other. Without my mom, I felt lost and disjointed from the rest of my family now. I feel I need to reconnect with my family and all things that keep me grounded. My dad is a country boy from deep Alabama. He never went past technical school, but that was the furthest anyone went to school in his generation or before. He and my mom instilled the importance of education in me. There was never a time when I even thought about anything else. For a lot of kids, there is a choice which you make around sixteen, which is will I go to college or not? That was never a question for me. That question never even crossed my mind. The only choice I ever remember making is what school I would go to. And my mom was so proud when I chose Morehouse College, the school of Martin Luther King. To this day, it makes me misty eyed to think about it. As I wipe a tear from my right eye, I dial my dad, and the phone rings several times. I finally hear a hello on the other end. It's the voice of an old black man. That scares me because I never thought of my dad as old; he was always strong and vital, hardworking, and full of laughter and real, simple, country values. Age is not something I think could ever conquer him, but it seems to have caught up with him.

"Hello Dad. It's JD."

"Jasper, is that you? Boy, you haven't returned any of my calls. I didn't know what happened to you. If I hadn't seen you on the news from time to time, I would have thought you were dead. How you doing boy?" And before I can answer, he proceeds to tell me what's been happening with my extended family for the last three years in detail. This aunt passed away. That nephew is in jail. This niece graduated from college.

I listen patiently, just ingraining his voice in my head. How could I have thought I was living a real life when everybody who gave two shits about me were cut out of it and isolated from me? What if I hadn't called him and he had died. How would I have felt if I had never heard his voice again or heard him say my name? What type of life is it to die alone? Is that what I wanted for my dad? More precisely is that what I wanted for myself? As I listen to him drone on, tears of joy drip down my face as I feel like I'm reconnecting with what's real and stepping away from the facsimile that my life has become.

After a time I tell him, "I love you, Dad."

He says. "JD, when are you gonna see your son? Your wife?"

"My ex-wife, Dad."

"As I said, your wife brought him by the house for Thanksgiving last year. He's growing to be a right handsome, strong young man. His momma tells me she has to beat the young girls off him with a stick. Just like you, JD."

"Not like me, Dad. Women never chased after me or wanted me. I was a pretty lonely guy throughout school. Women want me now but . . ."

"They don't want you boy. They want your money and your dumbass be giving it to them. Stop trying to be Captain Save-A-Ho and be a real man who handles his business."

"I'm trying Dad. I broke away from all the women I've been seeing. I've stopped drinking, and I'm drying out."

"That's a good step, boy, but ain't none of that permanent unless you make some drastic changes in your life. You see, boy, you have left some holes in your life by emptying the women and liquor out, but if you don't do something to change your life, the holes where those things were will remain, and you will fill them up with the same thing again or something just as bad.

"I've got my mind on it, Dad, and I'm gonna see what I can do. I love you Dad."

"I love you too, boy. Just be a man and everything will be ok. I didn't raise you to be no Captain Save-A-Ho."

I look at my watch. It's now midnight and I've got a thousand things to do tomorrow, cases to handle, people who want to retain me to work for them, and all I can think about is my family. After an hour of this, I sit up, swing my legs off the edge of the bed, and cradle my face in my hands. I can't do this. I'm not gonna be able to sustain. If I'm still in this bachelor pad, I'm never gonna be free of my hoeing ways. I must rid myself of this whoremongering spirit. I think of a future for myself that I'll be sixty years old and chasing 20 year old women. I don't want that for my life. I want to be sixty and sitting at the fireplace surrounded by my grandkids telling them stories and slipping them candy when their parents aren't looking. I want that for my life. I stand up and grab my Mike Vick jersey and worn down Levi's. I grab my brown leather jacket out of the closet and pick my keys off the counter and I get the hell out of that place. I go over to the garage and hop in my 840CI. As I hear the engine roar, I let it warm up. I ask myself where the hell am I going? Before I can answer myself, I know the answer. I drive out of the garage bust a left loop around Baltimore Street to McClellan and before you know it I'm on 95 South.

CHAPTER 21

Welcome home

I DRIVE THROUGH THE night drinking soda and alternating from the air conditioner to the heater to keep myself awake and alert. (I've never been a night person. I like sleep, too much). I pull up to my driveway at Lake Norman in North Cackalacky. Yep, I drove home. I'm so overwhelmed with excitement that even though the sun is still rising, I can't restrain myself and walk up to the front door. I knock and ring the doorbell for five minutes, and then I hear a rumbling and scratching at the door, then I hear a definitely irritated voice yell

"Who is it?!"

Then I hear the chain unlatch and the door unlock and the next thing I see is my wife (ex-wife) standing in her bathrobe and slippers with her hair wrapped in a scarf staring at me with groggy, pissed off eyes.

"Jasper, what are you doing here? And why the hell are you so early?" She ties her robe and steps out the door shutting it behind her. "You don't just come knocking at somebody's door his early. I have to go to work."

"You still commute to Duke?"

"No, I'm at UNC –Charlotte. They gave me a full professorship and I don't have to commute anymore. Is everything ok?" she asked all of sudden with a look of concern on her face. "Is your father all right? Oh please let him be ok JD. Jr. adores him" she raises her hand to her mouth and gasps.

"No he's fine. Everything is fine. I came to see you because I cleaned my life up and I need you and Jr. back in it."

The look of concern immediately goes from concerned to eternally pissed off just that quick. Uh oh, I'm in for it.

"How dare you? You selfish prick. You have ignored me and your son for five years and now you want to just hop back into our lives like nothing happened. You missed your son's basketball and baseball games. You missed explaining to him the birds and bees and most important you never gave him the image of what it means to be a man and you just want to hop in like it was a commercial break on tv?"

I stutter," I uh, I mean, I uh."

"You, what you stupid selfish motherfucker? And you think I would have you back. You think I would love you after you hurt me, left me shamed me by cheating on me with other women, and you think I can let you back in."

I do the only thing I can think to do. I rush up to her pick her off the ground and smother her ruby red lips with mine and for three seconds it was the most magical kiss in my life until I felt a ton of bricks come down on my left ear. I sat her down and I'm woozy and staggering like a prize fighter who is getting his ass kicked. My wife Stephanie yells: "JD this isn't a motherfuckin' movie. You don't get to just walk out of our lives, sow your oats, and walk back in ... life doesn't work like that. I then see tears streaming down her eyes."

"First you need to show if you can be a part of our lives for real. Show me you can be consistent and maybe I will think about letting you back into our lives."

I hear a young male voice with a deep baritone say," Is everything ok?"" Ah ha! That's what it is. She has another dude in there and she doesn't want her lover to see me. Let me fix this quick fast and in a hurry.

"Hey motherfucker come out here right now and face the music.. What the hell are you doing in my house?

Stephanie looks at me "Are you crazy? You don't really want to do this." I see the door open and a 6'4"young black man with a mini-fro walks out. He is about a good 230 and he looks real familiar... Stephanie wouldn't rob the cradle ... Oh, shit! I know why he looks so familiar ... it's my son. God how stupid I am. The JD, Jr. speaks.

"I don't appreciate you coming down here and bothering my mom like this ... "

"But son."

"No buts JD...I'm not gonna call you dad because you ain't no damn father you're a sperm donor. Don't bother us again or I'll beat your ass and then call the cops." He holds the door open for his mom who is fully enveloped in tears now and he wraps his arms around her as she cries on his chest and then he slams the door in my face. Damn, how do I make such a mess of everything around me? Why did I think I could just walk back in their lives like no big deal. I had missed my son transforming from a boy to a man. I had missed his highs and lows but most of all I had missed being there for him as a father figure. No woman and no drink were ever worth that. I walk back slowly to my car. I get in, shut the door, and I lean back and grip the steering wheel with the grip of death. Why do I have to be so impulsive? Why do I think that just my presence will make everything better? I'm afraid that my life is over and my family no longer needs me nor loves me. I turn my car and head towards 85 North I might as well head back home. As I drove and pulled on to the exit of 85 North, I all of a sudden slam my brakes and my car slips to a stop all of a sudden, so sudden that the three cars behind me almost wreck. A barrage of horns go off, so I pull off on to the shoulder. Dammit JD, stop being so impulsive. Since things didn't immediately go your way. You're gonna hop on the highway and leave. Go ahead little boy run away. Or are you ready to finally grow up? Show Stephanie you are a grown up. I bet you never knew my wife's name until just now... I guess it was too painful to mention because I know the evil that I have brought into her life. I look at my watch and see it is 10. I notice about 10 messages on my cell all from my office and from Jeff's cell he must be going crazy thinking I went off on a binge and all this new business that is knocking at the door is going to go away. I get onto the highway and pull off at the next exit where I see a grocery store. I walk into the store and I grab an apartment book that I see on the rack near the entrance. I walk back out to my car and just then my Blackberry buzzes again. A phone call, damn. Well I gotta do this sooner or later. "Hey, Jeff how's it going?"

"How's it going? How's it going?" he says are you trying to ruin this business? Where are you? Drunk in some hooker's apartment? Or are you on your way to jail?? Or are you in a hospital because you finally got caught by a jealous boyfriend? Where the fuck are you, JD?

I take a minute and gather myself. I hear Jeff yelling" Hello? Hello?"

"I've decided to move back to North Carolina. I'm trying to win my family back."

"Why the fuck are you so impulsive JD? Couldn't you have done this gradually? You didn't have to leave today. It wasn't like she was gonna let you back in the door since you been gone for so long (apparently everybody but me knew this).JD I've been a friend to you when nobody else would. I have a family to provide for and we are looking at more money than this firm has seen in three years...How can you walk away from that? "

I said "Like this "and hung up. God I'm a prick. How could I turn my back on my friend? I say this as I leaf through the apartment book. I stop on a page that shows a townhouse that really catches my eye. Three stories modeled after Brooklyn brownstones, but brand new and modern. Sounds damn good to me. I sit there for fifteen minutes and bang my hands on the steering wheel. I can't be two places at once. I can't be responsible for everybody. I wanted to open my own office down here and get to know my family again. As I sit there I start to feel stupid, isn't this the sort of reasons for airplanes? I call Jeff's cellphone back. He answers,

" What do you want cocksucker? "

I say, "Chill out bitch. I got a solution to all this."

"What bitch?"

"Have all the clients come in and patch me through on a conference call. They retain the firm and I handle the trial work, but we hire an associate to do the courtroom and daily drudge stuff. I open a branch of Davis and Stephenson in Charlotte and we divvy up the money from the new cases."

"JD, you're my boy"

"Jeff, you my nigga"

We verbally slap five and hang up. Soon, I'm on my way to the realtor's office.

Now since the depression caused by the Bushes, Charlotte is a different place. .Charlotte was a bank boomtown where two of the ten largest banks in the US were headquartered--- .Wachovia and Bank of America. If you read any papers at all, you will know that Wachovia failed and was bought by Wells Fargo. Bank of America bought of a piece of the banking mess (Merrill Lynch) that it was unable to digest smoothly. All this changed the boomtown to a ghost town. Foreclosures are everywhere. The playhouses of rich bankers and the rich merchants that serviced them are empty. The townhouse condos and homes of everyone in town are affected. All of this is good news for me because that means I could get a great price on a townhome or apartment. As I drive to the realtor, I give them my information. One person recognizes me as the lawyer that was on TV with that murder case in Baltimore. They seemed pleased as punch when I tell them I'm moving to town. The office boss actually takes over my interview. His name is Jack Sharp. He's a heavyset black man with a bald head but still hair populated on the sides of his head. You know the George Jefferson look. As we sit down, he tells me he has the perfect place for me, a three bed townhouse whose lower level is a business office store front. I'm immediately intrigued. He gives me the key, a map and directions, and says take all the time you need. Just bring me the key back today or tomorrow. Just take your time. I immediately drive over to it. It's in an area of uptown that is pretty nice, sidewalks with tree lined streets. Seems like a good amount of foot traffic and the federal court. I can see just down the street. I walk inside the building and there are polished hardwood floors everywhere. There are plantation shutters.. Light tan painted walls.. And a marble entrance way. As I go up the stairs to the living area, I'm floored by the subzero kitchen equipment and the mahogany cabinets. Wow this place would be millions in Baltimore! I look at the spec sheet and see they want $2500 per month for rent but the place is for sale for $189,999. I'm no fool, if I can get this place for that price I'm gonna do it. What better way to show Stephanie that I'm gonna be permanent in their lives than buying a place and sticking to it. I walk out the front door. I love the place. I look down the street the other direction and low and behold there is a strip club 4 blocks away. Aww shit! Do I need the temptation? Well the reality is that whether it's 4 blocks or next door, it doesn't mean I have to go there and spend my money there. I'm never going to be able to avoid seeing the existence of strip clubs, but that doesn't mean I have to go in and partake. But you can bet I'm gonna use the presence of that place to drop the cost of this place substantially.

Later that afternoon with a contract of sale in my pocket for my new town house, I drive back towards my house. I mean my wife's house. I stop five minutes away and call her. She picks up the phone.

"Hi?"

"Hi, Stephanie. I just want to apologize about the scene I caused this morning. I want to let you know that I love you and I'm going to be a permanent part of Junior's life and I'd like to be a part of yours as well."

'Hmm… we will see JD. I am surprised you haven't found a woman to lay up with already."

"That's not what I want anymore. I'm too old for that and I know what I want for myself and my life and whoremongering ain't it."

"Well, if you're interested this Sunday you can come over to dinner and we can talk and you can see your son."

That's fine I just got a contract on a townhouse and I'm setting up my Charlotte office starting next week. I'm gonna fly out this evening and wrap up the business I need to in Baltimore, so I can start my life here fresh and new. I 'll fly back on Sunday morning."

"Humph you sure something won't come up and you'll be working late and need to stay... I don't want to break your son's heart again about your bullshit."

"No, Stephanie. That's not gonna happen. I love y'all. I'm five minutes away. Can I just come get a goodbye hug before I go to the airport? "

"Humph, make it quick I got stuff to do."

I hop in the 840 and tear out of there like a bat out of hell. I arrive at the house in three minutes. I see Stephanie at the door. Her hair is down and her makeup is on. God, she is just as pretty as she was at twenty two at forty. Jesus what the fuck did I leave?

I walk up to her. Hug her and she hugs back. "Please just be there for your son. Don't worry about me. "I look down at her not releasing her from my arms.

"Don't worry you are both my responsibility and I'm never gonna leave you ever again. Hey, I got something to show you. I pull out the contract of sale. I just went into contract on a townhouse for my business and to live here so I can be near y'all."

She smiles through her tears and says, "Hurry up and go. You are gonna miss your flight."

I kiss her forehead but she stops me. "No more forehead kisses; that's you using your slickness on me just hug me ok?"

I say, "Yes Ma'am" and squeeze for all I'm worth. I walk back to the car and drive off with a song in my head "I Apologize" by Tank)' I turn my car onto the road and a few minutes I turn into the airport parking lot. In less than two hours, I land at BWI Airport.

CHAPTER 22

Reflections on my life

AS I WALK TO THE BWI light rail stop I feel kind of nervous, like I'm returning to the scene of the crime. I get on the train which is full of airport workers heading home. I grab a seat in the front of the train and in about 20 minutes I'm in downtown Baltimore across from my old apartment building. I turn away and head directly to the office. It takes me five minutes to arrive there and the office is in an uproar. Clients are everywhere. Activity is good for a law office it means we can pay our bills and buy our kids GI Joe with the Kung Fu grip. I walk over to Jeff's office I see him counting a cash retainer and giving a receipt to the client. I wait till he acknowledges me and walks over to my office. I sit there and my assistant Christy walks in.

"Hi, JD. Do you want your medicine? It's been a long time since I took care of daddy. "She licks her lips lasciviously. I shake my head.

" No thanks, Christy. I'm headed in another direction in life. I don't want to do those things anymore."

"You don't want sex anymore. EWWW I heard about this on Jerry Springer. Men that have so much sex that they turn gay... JD How could you? "Christy I'm not gay I'm just gonna be faithful to my wife.

"Wife? JD, you are divorced!!!"

"But I'm hoping not to stay that way. I need sex just like the next man, but I can't have meaningless sex anymore. I want it to be with love and caring . Christy you're a good friend but that's it .You've got a husband who loves you . You're better than sucking my dick on demand. I value you more and you should value yourself more."

"Fine I'll go see if Jeff needs his medicine since you must have turned into a faggot. "She walks out angrily and slams the door so hard the stuff on my desk shakes. As soon as she's gone, Jeff pops in.

"JD. What's shaking baby ? We are gonna be rich . I've taken in 350,000 in cash fees the last two days for clients that want you to represent them.

"That's great Jeff. Hey, Can I ask you a question?"

"Yeah, sure."

"Are you having sex with Christy?"

"Well I wouldn't call it sex. She just slobs the knob every once in a while."

I look at Jeff amazed . " But you're a happy family man."

"Everybody needs to get the pipes blown out every once in a while. "

"Jeff, you're gonna lose everything you hold dear because that is a slippery slope that I stumbled down and I don't want the same thing to happen to you."

"What are you talking about man? Who are you to judge me? You have been a habitual cheater and now you're judging me?".

"I'm not judging you Jeff . I'm actually sad for you because my filth and depravity has rubbed off on you. You're going to have to learn a hard lesson. "

"What lesson is that?"

"That there is no such thing as casual sex .. It feels like the real thing. It tastes and smells like the real thing . But it's not. It's like a piece of paper sent by fax. Even though it copies the original, it is not the original it doesn't have the spirit and passion and love and essence of the real thing. If you get used to the fake one you will never have the real one. I learned that when I lost my family and I can't be around when I see you lose the same thing. Best friend or not I will not be touched by its taint again. Return those retainers I'm not going to do those cases and I 'm not going to open Davis and Stephenson in Charlotte. I'm going to do my own thing."

"Goodbye Jeff. "

"Yo JD, don't do this bro. I need this money"

"And I need to be free of the life you're living and I will not subject myself or my family to it. I'm sorry Jeff but I'm gone. I drop the office key on the floor as I walk out. I turn and give Jeff my condo key as I leave. I was going to sell this place but I guess you're going to be needing this in the not too distant future."

As I leave the building, I see Jeff's wife Lauren storming in to the building.

"Where is that bastard? He gave me chlamydia. How the hell could my husband cheat on me?"

"I think he's in my office Lauren. Goodbye."

"This is your fault JD. I should have never let my husband work with a whore like you...."

As I leave, I hail a cab and call Southwest on my Blackberry and schedule a flight back to Charlotte. As I am sitting in the back of the cab, I'm wondering, since I got back early whether I can convince Stephanie to let me take her and Junior to see the Bobcats play against Cleveland and King James tomorrow night. I bet she'll be surprised I never came home early before it was always late. As the cab pulls on to the 85 South part of Baltimore, I smile and look back and know that I'm headed to a real life and not the reasonable facsimile I lived in Baltimore. It's time for real life and home. I like the sound of that. I lay back and relax and the theme music in my head is Bob Marley's Redemption Song.

www.ingramcontent.com/pod-product-compliance
Lightning Source LLC
Chambersburg PA
CBHW060815120626
46557CB00001B/232